Sarah's social visit is about to challenge her moral standards.

"Obviously you don't need much time to learn music. It must come very naturally to you," Mrs. Winston smiled, handing her another cup of coffee.

Sarah blushed. "I've always loved to sing. I guess just doing it for so long makes me able to learn new things quickly. Of course, this piece isn't exactly new to me."

A light rap came on the door, so faint Sarah wasn't sure she'd heard it. *It's certainly late for visitors,* she thought. *I hope it isn't Papa come to find me!* She flushed at the embarrassing thought.

"Who's there?" called Mr. Winston, starting for the door.

"Friend of a frien'," came the tentative voice from outside the hallway entrance.

Mr. Winston stopped, his outreached arm faltering at the parlor doorway. His wife put a hand to her mouth. Even young Joanna looked at Sarah oddly. In fact, Sarah suddenly found herself the center of a circle of frightened, uncertain eyes.

"Don't worry about Sarah, Father," David finally said. "Besides, you haven't much choice."

Bewildered, Sarah watched as Charles Winston nodded and went out to open the door. Through the parlor entrance they could see a young colored woman nearly collapse into the hallway, a sleeping child in her arms.

"Come in. You're among friends."

JILL RICHARDSON makes her home in Minnesota with her husband and three young children. *Friend of a Friend* is her first inspirational romance novel.

Friend of a Friend

Jill Richardson

Heartsong Presents

ACKNOWLEDGEMENTS

This has been a project for which many have given their time and assistance. I greatly appreciate the help of the reference librarians at Anoka County libraries. They are terrific people! Shirley Durie and the others at Alton Historical Society were also of great help and showed such a delighted willingness to be of service. Thank you to Lucille, Anita, Lanay, and Barb for many hours of constructive criticism. Especially thank you to my husband Brent for his steadfast belief that I could do anything. After all, how could I write a love story without him?

DEDICATION

To Rebecca and Emily, two of the best "choices" I ever made.

A note from the Author:
I love to hear from my readers! You may write to me at the following address: **Jill Richardson**
Author Relations
P.O. Box 719
Uhrichsville, OH 44683

ISBN 1-55748-896-7

FRIEND OF A FRIEND

Cover illustration by Kay Salem.

PRINTED IN THE U.S.A.

one

"Achoo!" A cloud of dust descended on the head of a young woman who seemed already a little worse for her day's experience. The long brown curls she had carefully tucked beneath a scarf had escaped. They now hung about her face and neck, haloed with cobwebs and clinging to her in the July heat. She stood on tiptoe and strained her arm holding the wet cloth, but she could not reach the window, high above the shelves in front of her. She had only managed to knock the dust from the top shelf onto her head.

"Oh, where do I even start?" she moaned. "It's a good thing I saved this old brown dress." The dress, like the lean-to in which she stood, had seen better days. It was also much too warm for a southern Illinois summer. *But,* thought Sarah, surveying the scene around her, *no other clothing would do for this chore.*

She wiped her dusty hands on the dress and turned them over to look at them. Under the dirt she could see two blisters already showing and others threatening to form. Her carefully manicured fingernails showed the cracks and jagged edges of a week of hard work. "To think," she said, holding her hands in front of her, "one week of being a 'pioneer woman' can undo twenty years of pampered existence."

For the past week, Sarah Brown had scrubbed, dusted, polished, and repaired seemingly every corner of the big old house her father had bought such a short time ago. Six years of neglect, vandals, and harsh weather—with no inhabitants to repair the damage—had left a mark on the place she wasn't sure she could erase. Of course, had the house been livable, Papa couldn't have gotten it for so little. Land was not nearly so dear here in frontier

Illinois as it was back home, and the heir of this big old dustbin had just wanted to be rid of it quickly. With her father conducting business and her younger sister off finding new friends, the task of making their new house habitable fell to Sarah.

"Why, Papa, did you buy this place?" She directed her question at the cracked flowerpots before her, whose occupants had long since given up their effort at life. "It's not as if we need the space anymore, with only three of us. Mama and Anne are both gone. Couldn't we have gotten a smaller, cozier house that didn't need to be completely redone, inside and out?" But she shook her head even as she said the words. Gerald Brown would never live in anything but grand style. And she had to admit the place had once been both grand and stylish. *Never mind if the walls are crumbling about our ears now,* she thought wryly, taking another swipe at the dusty shelves. *It's a large enough house that we won't look as poor as we are. That's all Papa needs.*

If the house looked frightening, the lean-to she now occupied defied description. A blanket of dust lay everywhere, so thick she could probably sleep on it. Rusty tools she'd wager had never been used on this house and garden huddled in a neglected heap. She approached a cob-webbed corner with trepidation. It was hard to believe anything could live in that place, but she'd much rather not test the assumption. As if to prove her point, a fat black spider scuttled out of the webs and up the wall.

"Aaah!" Sarah jumped backward. Unfortunately, she only succeeded in dislodging another shower of dust as she hit the post behind her.

"Sarah!" her father's voice boomed from in front of the house. "Where are you? We've got visitors!"

"Oh, dear," she groaned. "That's just what the day needed. Company—and I look worse than the beggars I used to see on the city corners." *Oh, well,* she thought. *It's probably only the local pastor or a neighborly grandma.* Unwinding the scarf, she patted her hair and wiped the dust she could from her face and dress.

"Coming, Papa!" she called.

Rounding the corner to the front of the house, Sarah halted. The two strangers before her bore no resemblance to grandmothers. A man about her father's age stood in conversation with him, while the young man at his side seemed to be eyeing the remains of forlorn gardens around him.

That they were father and son she had no doubt. The gray in the older man's hair didn't hide the dark brown hue that matched his son's. He was of average height, the other slightly taller. *Certainly not area farmers,* Sarah thought, judging by their clothing. The father's dark coat and vest proclaimed him a prosperous businessman. Puzzled, she went forward to meet the new acquaintances.

"Dear Lord, girl, where have you been?"

Sarah winced at her father's language. She would never get used to the way he spoke her Lord's name.

"I've been trying to clean the shed, Papa, as I told you I would be. I'm very sorry for my somewhat disheveled appearance." She smiled as she addressed the two men. "But the Bible says the rain falls on all men alike, and so it is with dust and dirt. They have no consideration at all."

"There are servants for that sort of thing," Papa fumed.

"There are?" she inquired. "Well, if you see any about the place, do send them over."

Her father's set jaw and look silenced his daughter. She knew he was angry at her appearance in front of strangers—important strangers too, if she judged correctly. She shouldn't have tried to be humorous—he clearly didn't find the situation amusing. For Gerald Brown's daughter to appear in public looking as if she had to work! It was an unpardonable offense she was sure she'd hear about later.

"Sarah, this is Mr. Charles Winston and his son, David."

She smiled at the pair, recovering her poise.

"Good afternoon. It's nice to have neighbors visit so soon."

"Pleased to meet you, Miss Brown," said the older man.

"Very pleased," echoed his son. "I wonder if you mean to imply we come too soon and should have given you good warning," he added, arching eyebrows over laughing hazel eyes that surveyed her dusty hair and dress.

"Not at all," she retorted. "In fact, you should have come sooner. Yesterday I swept the chimney!" she announced, her brown eyes sparkling back with mischief.

"You did not!" her papa thundered. "No daughter of mine. . . ."

"Of course not, Papa. They know I was only having fun. Truly," she said turning back to them, "you are welcome. Won't you come inside?"

"Thank you, but this isn't purely a social call. I want to talk business with your father. Actually, I've been doing some business with him for years, but now that you're out west, we're finally meeting."

"You won't be needing me, will you, Father? I might stay out here and, ah, help clean chimneys."

Mr. Winston waved his hand in acceptance as the two older men moved toward the house. "Business talk is boring for you young people, I know. Can't say as I blame you though."

Sarah turned back into the yard. "You're too late for chimneys. I told you, that was yesterday."

"What rotten luck. Still, there must be some mess left I can get into."

"Several, Mr. Winston, as you can see," she replied, waving her hand to encompass the yard and house. They strode toward the old wooden well that, like everything else, needed visible repair. At least she could draw some water to clean her hands and face.

"I've always been sorry to see the old Crandall place look so. . . uninhabited," he said. "It was once such a beautiful, lively house. Of course, I don't remember the owners very well. Their children were all grown and gone before I was older, so we didn't meet much. Still, most people loved old Mrs. Crandall and her house."

"What happened?"

"She died about eight years ago. Just seemed like her husband didn't have much left to care for after that. He tried to hang on to the house, but with no one there, no one to enjoy the flower garden or fill all those rooms, well, he just couldn't bring himself to care, I suppose. The house started falling down around him, and he packed up to go live with a daughter. That was a while back. I had heard he died recently—that must be why this place went up for sale."

"I'm glad to know someone else was happy in it once. That makes the task seem less. . .formidable."

"It must be quite a change from your home in. . .Washington, I think your father said?"

"Yes, that's always been home. And it certainly is a change." *In more ways than one,* she thought sadly, remembering her clean, bright city home and gentle elder sister a half-continent away. "But Papa. . .wanted to try his hand at the frontier. So here we are." She paused to pluck a struggling daisy from the tangle that had taken over the gardens.

"How did your mother like the idea?"

Sarah looked down. "Mama. . .died a few years ago. And my older sister, Anne, married and stayed behind. So it's only Papa, Margaret, and I who undertook to brave the savages." She smiled. "Or so everyone back east informed us you were."

"Oh. I'm very sorry. About your mother, that is. But I hope you'll find us savages to your liking."

"I'm sure I will. I already like the open space. City life can be so confining."

"My parents moved here when Illinois first became a state—not many years after they were married. So I've never known any life but this. Been to New York once, but. . .we like it here in the West."

"I am rather looking forward to it, actually," she answered.

"Although in truth, this part of the change hasn't been much fun." Sarah pulled an exaggerated frown, looking again at her hands.

"Your father gave us to understand no proper eastern lady would dirty her hands cleaning a house."

"Papa would give me to understand that too, if he could. Unfortunately he no longer. . . . Well, someone must do it at any rate," she finished, biting off what she had been about to confide. By this time they had reached the well, and she began lowering a bucket into its cool depths.

"Here, let me help you," he offered, taking the rope and handle. "I expect you've had to haul several buckets of water over the past week or so. My sister and her husband thought of organizing some people to come over and help, when we heard someone had moved in, but well, sometimes it's best to meet strangers first. Some people don't take kindly to what they consider a mixture of meddling and charity."

"I wouldn't mind a little charity!" Sarah laughed, looking at the garden in front of her and remembering to whose hands its repair too would fall. Then she sobered. "But Papa, I think, might prefer to maintain his dignity. Anyway, it keeps me busy." She smiled. "Your father said he does business with Papa. What sort of business is he in?"

"He runs the two mills in town. He's also bought a great deal of interest in the new Chicago-Alton railroad. I suspect that, not the mill, is what he's talking to Mr. Brown about. Your father is in shipping, I believe?" She nodded. "If, between them, they could forge a freight agreement up the Mississippi and then to Chicago, I think both would be very pleased."

"I'm sure. Yes, Papa ran some Yankee clippers back east. When steam came in, he bought a very small line running between Alton and New Orleans. He's often a very astute businessman. He knew then that steam was the future, both on land and sea. He jumped in as soon as they broke the steamboat monopoly on the Mississippi in 'twenty-four." Sarah felt more grateful than David Winston knew for this piece of foresight on her father's part. It was all they had left now.

"He must have built it up pretty well then over the years."

"Yes—several ships and a warehouse here by now. It started quite small—just one steamer. Or so he tells me." She began trying to scrub the dirt off her hands with the cool well water.

"So what made him want to move way out here? He must have had more work on the coast than he could ever need."

"He. . .he just. . .wanted a change. A new challenge, you know." She jumped up from the well and started for the porch.

"Tell me something about your town. What should a new person here know?" she asked.

"There isn't much to tell," he said, starting after her. "We're kind of standard as towns go. It's been settled for a while, though we only became the official 'city of Alton' back in 'thirty-seven. Lots of nice people. A few barely tolerable."

She smiled.

"You'll find the usual assortment of churches and saloons. Of course, being good Methodists, we only frequent the former." He grinned at her. "For any purchases, Green's store is nearest you. Despite the name, it's run by Liza O'Reilly. Used to be Liza Green. Her father gave the store to her when she married, providing she kept the name. And the most important thing I can tell you about her is—don't tell her anything you don't want us all to know."

She laughed, "I'll remember that. You make it sound like a pleasant place. I can't wait to get out and explore. But before I meet any new people I have to make sure I wouldn't be embarrassed to invite them into my house!"

"But you've met two new people here today."

"And one of them is in my house. So it can't truly be so bad. But I want it to be perfectly home, and it's not yet that, of course."

They reached the porch and sat down on the top step. "But this town is central for shipping—you mentioned that," she said. "Because of the river?"

"Because of two rivers—the Mississippi and the Missouri meet right here. Most of what's up the Missouri is still pretty wild country, but it stretches for a long way, and it will be very important when the land is settled. There'll be more goods coming and going through here than your father can handle— he chose well."

Just then the two men emerged from the house, shaking hands. "Get back in touch when I work out the details," Sarah's father said. "Glad to meet you."

"The same," said Mr. Winston, climbing into his buggy as his son followed. "By the way, thought we might invite you out to church Sunday, if you've not decided on one yet. Right over on the corner of Liberty and Fourth. Ten o'clock, Sunday."

Sarah brightened. "Oh! I've missed church so. . . ."

"Well," her papa interrupted. "We'll see. We'll see. Kind of busy around here right now. Just moving in and all, you know. But we'll be seeing you soon."

With this noncommittal response, the two men drove off. *Church!* thought Sarah. Not since they left home had she been to church. It hadn't been that long, but she missed it, especially here, where she knew no one. Papa wouldn't go, she knew, but she would. It would be a first step toward making this strange place her home.

two

Saturday morning found Sarah back in the lean-to, putting finishing touches on her project. The walls didn't precisely gleam, but they were clean. She had hauled most of the rusty tools and old flowerpots away. Now her own gardening equipment stood organized on the newly dusted shelves. Her tools were few—those her mother had used on a small, prized corner of their land back home. Sarah had never actually used any of them herself, but she had wanted to keep them.

With light coming through the clean window again, she could see that her work would do.

Backing up for one last surveillance, she tripped. "Ouch! What was that?" She bent down to look closely and discovered a small recess carved into one of the floorboards. Sliding her fingers under it, she pulled up. To her surprise, several boards came up to form a door, revealing a short ladder and a tiny, black room. "What a strange thing to put out here." She wrinkled her forehead in puzzlement. "Is it a cellar?" she wondered aloud, peering into the darkness. "But the house already has one." Descending the ladder, she dimly saw several ropes suspended cross the ceiling. On one, bunches of butterfly weed, everlasting, and bugbane still hung. "A drying room!" she cried, amazed. "So someone did once care for this house and garden. These must have been some of the last flowers Mrs. Crandall cut before she died." Standing in the darkness, Sarah felt suddenly closer to the unknown woman who had loved beautiful things and been loved in return. Well, so it would be again. She would bring flowers back to this room.

"But now, I must get cleaned up and see if I can find that

church. It wouldn't do to get lost tomorrow and be late. Maybe I'll pick my first bunch of daisies and buttercups on the way." Just the thought of worshiping with others on the following day made her move faster toward the house. She hummed a favorite hymn while she washed.

Once she began walking, the summer afternoon sun made her glad she had worn her lightest muslin dress. Even its cream-colored folds with all the petticoats underneath felt sticky after only a few minutes. "Ick. The heat is worse than home," she grumbled. Then she remembered. "No, this is home now. There's no good in making comparisons." By the time she reached the nearby general store, her curls clung to her face with the dampness.

The yet-unknown Liza O'Reilly stood on her porch, surveying the street. Waving at her, Sarah noticed a yellow paper flapping on the store post. Curious, she drew nearer to read it.

ONE-HUNDRED-DOLLAR REWARD. Runaway, Negro man named Josiah. 25 years. Stocky build, very black. Lash marks on back and missing a piece of his left ear. FIFTY DOLLARS for proof he's dead. Mr. J. Delhaney, Jefferson County.

A familiar sick feeling washed over her. She had seen many of these papers back home. She recognized the stick figure of a runaway slave and cringed at the reward, often as much for a dead man as for a living one. Descriptions of men and women showed they'd been whipped and branded as if they were cattle. Though the nation's capital, where she once lived, was a slave district, Sarah shared her mother's abhorrence of people owning other people. She had believed she was leaving that behind when they had moved to a free state. Then what was this flyer doing here?

Backing away, she noticed the group of men gathered on the porch, alternately talking and spitting into a large sawdust barrel.

"Think you kin catch that slave, Jake? Or d'ye s'pose he's gone too far by now?"

"Ain't no slave too far for my hounds, Abel. You know that.

I got men out lookin' for 'im now. Jest hope we don't get no trouble out o' him. D'ruther have the hundred than the fifty, but I got to take what I kin get. . . ." The man speaking shrugged his big shoulders as the group laughed. Sarah hurried on before they could notice her. The conversation left her with a feeling of uncertain dread. Maybe finding the church would drive away this cold feeling.

The simple brown church, when Sarah reached it, appealed to her. Its plain board construction with a rough wooden cross atop it seemed more in harmony with Jesus' humble beginnings than the huge brick edifices she was used to seeing. Of course, they had their beauty too. After all, she reasoned, the people in it mattered to God, not the building. But something about the place's simplicity fit with her new life. She felt warmly invited by its unassuming peace.

"Well, now I can find my way, and I know about how long it takes to get here." She spoke to herself, turning to survey the dusty streets she would have to walk again to return home. "I guess I'm all ready for tomorrow. But right now I'm hot and tired!" Spying a nearby tree, she sat down in the shade beneath it and let a welcome breeze skim across her face. "Oh, that feels so wonderful," she sighed. "I'll just close my eyes for a minute and then start back. . . ."

&

"You're a little early. Services don't start until tomorrow morning."

Sarah's startled eyes flew open. "What? Where. . . ?" She flushed, recognizing David Winston in the buggy above her.

"I. . .I must have fallen asleep." She struggled to her feet.

"Well, so long as you don't do so in the service tomorrow morning." He smiled down at her red face.

"No, I'm sure I won't." She straightened her dress, trying to quiet her embarrassment. "I just decided to walk over to make sure I could find the way. It was such a warm walk. I guess I was more tired than I knew."

"If you can wait a few minutes, I'll take you home. I promised my sister I'd come by to get some air into the place before tomorrow. But that won't take more than a minute or two." He leaped down from the seat and fastened the reins to a tree limb.

"Your sister?"

"Guess we didn't tell you yesterday. Her husband's the minister here. Actually, he was the minister before he was her husband. Now he seems quite happy to be both," he said, opening the door for them to go inside. With each one working down one side of the room, they soon had breezes blowing through the windows that lined the walls.

"There. It will be a little cooler in here tomorrow. Have to close them tonight though, or it'll also be full of mosquitoes. July around here can sure feel like the inside of a coal stove. The only thing good about it is that August is worse!" They returned to the bright sunlight outside. "Thanks for the help. Are you going home?"

"Yes. It's getting late. I'd better get back to see about supper." She gratefully accepted his hand into the buggy. "I do appreciate your saving me the hot walk home."

"Think you can find your way in the morning?" he asked, giving his horses the go-ahead sign.

"Oh, I think so. I just wanted to be sure. I don't know my way around very well yet. But I'll learn."

"It must be very different from your home. A big city, on the coast. Always bustling with important business. Alton's just a tiny town on a big river. We probably seem pretty dull here to you."

"Dull? To be here on the frontier, envisioning the future's big cities? Oh, no!" She gazed toward the riverfront. "There are dreams here—I can feel them all around. You're building something. That's always exciting." She paused. "I guess it depends on what you call dull. Sometimes I think dull is being where all the dreams and work are finished. But to have a dream—to see a goal ahead of me and know that was my reason to be here. How could life ever be dull then, anywhere?"

She didn't realize she was speaking so fervently until she saw his intense look. "I suppose that sounds silly," she finished, looking away.

"No indeed. We all need dreams to survive. 'Without vision the people perish,' God's Word tells us. If we're never reaching for what we envision, we'll never actually get ahold of anything. We'll just die right where we're standing."

"Yes," she said, surprised someone else could understand what she had meant. "Only. . .well maybe ordinary people don't get those kinds of visions. Maybe some of us just weren't meant to get ahold of much," she sighed.

"Well, I suppose that depends on what you're looking to get ahold of—and who you consider ordinary. I've known a lot of 'ordinary' people who were able to do amazing things with the Lord helping them. Not newsmaking achievements maybe, but amazing nonetheless. What is it you want to reach for?"

"I don't know. And I doubt very much Papa would appreciate any attempt to find out." She laughed slightly, shaking her head.

"Well, whatever it is, you'll find it if you care that greatly. Don't worry too much about it. If you're looking at all, you're ahead of a lot of people."

They fell silent for a while. Now that she was not walking, Sarah enjoyed the summer sunshine. She looked around her, trying to learn the new places they went by. Houses and businesses intermingled for a while, thinning out toward her own home on the town's outskirts. She felt glad, suddenly, for the big old house. It offered free space these houses didn't. *This city girl,* she thought, *is going to enjoy the country.* She noticed a cheerful blue patch by the roadside. "Such pretty blue flowers there. What are they?"

"Chickory. People around here mostly feel they're more weeds than flowers. But folks down South say they make a great cup of coffee."

His reference to the South reminded her. "Can I ask you something? I saw a flyer for a runaway slave on Green's general store. There was a group of men discussing it, talking about catching him."

"Who was it talking?" he asked quickly.

"Well, I didn't know any of them, of course. I remember two of them referring to each other as Jake and Abel." She shuddered, recalling the two men's cruel remarks. "That's all I know. Do men really make a business here of capturing runaway slaves? I thought Illinois was a free state."

"A brisk business, Sarah. Very brisk. We're right across the river from Missouri, remember. And not that far from Kentucky, though runaways from there wouldn't likely come this far west."

"But I thought people from free states helped them escape."

He looked at her measuringly. "People in some states do. People in this part of Illinois don't. Not considered good for one's health and family."

"But. . . ."

"I'm glad you found the church all right. I think you'll like it. It's not very big, but it's friendly, and we have good preaching. Even if the preacher is related to me," he laughed. He brought the team to a halt at her door. "Will we be meeting your sister tomorrow?"

"Um, no, I don't think so," she said, confused by the abrupt change of subject. "Margaret isn't likely to attend. I'm afraid I'll be alone."

"Then you can sit with us. You'll meet the rest of the family—and a number of others who are always eager to greet someone new. See you tomorrow."

"Yes, tomorrow," she answered, climbing to the ground. As she turned to the house, Sarah felt puzzled, more so because she couldn't say just why.

three

As if speaking of her made her appear, Margaret Brown stepped out the door as David pulled away. Sarah watched as her sister bounced down the steps, her auburn curls bouncing with her and flying free. *Never one to go slowly when faster will do,* she thought. Not for the first time, she realized how quickly her younger sister was growing up. Sixteen already! And by the looks of it, she'd soon outstrip her elder sister in height. Sarah shook her head, marveling at how unalike they were. Sarah favored her mother, with her warm brown hair and eyes and her calm progression through life. Margaret had inherited her father's brown-red hair, snapping green eyes, and tall, slender build. *And his temperament,* Sarah thought with a pang. She sighed at the idea of piloting such a volatile girl into young womanhood.

"Who was that?" her sister asked, gazing at the retreating buggy.

"Someone Papa and I met yesterday. His family invited us to church tomorrow. Would you like to go with me?"

"Oh, no. I've got better things to do on a summer Sunday morning."

"Suit yourself," Sarah replied, knowing full well her sister would do so anyway.

"But he's just handsome enough to make a girl consider it!"

"That's not why one goes to church," Sarah reproved. *Though,* she thought an instant later, *if it got Margaret in the door, might any reason do?*

"No, I suppose not. Besides, I'll bet he's a stuffy old man in that case. Too bad."

"Oh, yes. I'm sure he's doddering well into at least twenty-four or -five by now," Sarah laughed. "Soon he'll need a cane and

19

insist on bed by seven."

"Oh, Sarah, you know what I mean."

Sarah smiled. "You'll want that on," she said, pointing to her sister's bonnet, characteristically swinging from her hand. "It's hot on the road."

"Nasty weather," Margaret complained, tying the yellow bonnet rather insecurely on her head. "That's one good thing about moving west," she reasoned, playing with the ribbons. "These old clothes that would be hopelessly out of style back home look practically new here." She flipped the ribbons back and started walking toward the road. "Well, I'll see you later tonight."

"Wait. . . . Where are you going?"

"Down to Harriet Anderson's. She's a new friend I met a couple of days ago. They live in a big house on the bluff. She invited me to come watch the boats race today."

"They have boat races here? What sort?"

"Well, not a real, official race. The boats that come in to haul things sometimes race each other. Harriet says that only one boat can dock at a time, because there isn't enough space. This is such a tiny place," she groaned. "Anyway, the first one in gets everything that's waiting to go up or down the river. So when more than one come in, they race! She says it's so exciting. Everyone goes out to watch. The houses have decks built right on their roofs just for that reason! They're expecting three today!"

"Sounds dangerous to me." Sarah frowned, then relented at Margaret's pout. "Oh, dear, do I sound like a stuffy old lady? Yes, I imagine it would be thrilling to watch. I guess life isn't much fun if it's not scary once in a while."

Margaret waved good-bye and bounced off down the road. Sarah watched her go and sighed. It was true. She was getting stuffy. Forever plodding along by foot when the rest of the world raced by via steamboat. What was it David had said? "If we're never reaching for what we envision, we'll never actually get ahold of anything." What was she reaching for? Perhaps she'd never know unless she stopped clutching what she had.

Well, at any rate, she thought, mounting the steps to the house, *I can reach for some pots and pans and get some supper cooking.* Which, she realized, Margaret obviously wouldn't be home for. *How many times in the last few months,* she wondered, *did that happen? When did we stop having the family together at supper?*

"Oh, Mama, how I wish you were still here." She sighed again, tying on her apron. "You held us together, didn't you? And we never even knew. I've tried, Mama. I've really tried." Sarah smiled wistfully at the silliness of carrying on a conversation with her mother. But often, when it seemed Papa and Margaret didn't understand her, she found comfort in talking to the gentle woman she so missed.

"But Margaret's growing up and, like Papa, I'm afraid she's a little. . .headstrong. I can't make her obey me as I could when she was twelve. As you could. She goes her own way, and Papa, well, they're so much alike. I'm afraid he can't see the danger in it."

Of course, she thought wryly, *if foresight were one of Papa's greater gifts, we wouldn't be where we are.* Carefully, she began to chop the carrots and potatoes for the evening's stew, while her mind traveled far away. She remembered again their large, pillared home in the nation's capital. Servants had made their supper then, not Sarah or her mother. "It was a good thing you made sure I learned how, Mama," Sarah said. "God has a way of preparing us for everything." They had been one of the few families with paid servants instead of slaves. Papa was stubborn, but Mama's silent strength had usually gained the day. She had absolutely refused to call a human being her property.

Slowly, though, they had lost those servants and then their home. No one realized how much Sarah's mother had kept a quiet control of the household until she was gone. Papa had a thriving business up and down the coast, but it was Mama who made sure they never exceeded their income. Her father was a brilliant businessman, but he had no idea how to handle his own household affairs. Never had he known, or cared, about day-to-day workings. When his wife died, he cared even less.

Grieving over his loss, he had spent recklessly and was heedless of his business. After a while, that recklessness became habit. By the time he realized the seriousness of their situation, there were few options left. At the end of three years, the small side business he owned at the meeting of the Missouri and Mississippi rivers in Alton, Illinois, was all that was left. So they sold the house, packed what they still possessed, and moved west.

Sarah could have stayed with her newly married sister, Anne. But though she dearly loved and missed her older sister, she knew three would be too many for a couple just starting out. Besides, someone must care for Papa and Margaret.

"So here we are, Mama, and I'm taking care of them, just as you asked me to," she said, poking at the fire she had just started in the stove. "But I'm going to need a lot of wisdom. Papa wants me to be something I can't be—and I don't know how. He can't bear not being wealthy anymore. Or at least, he can't bear anyone else knowing he isn't."

She grimaced, remembering his displeasure yesterday. Luckily, his business arrangement with Mr. Winston had appeased his anger at her for "appearing in public like a maidservant." That description had been his only comment at supper last night.

She finished chopping the last of the vegetables and tossed them in the big black pot.

"I can't deceive people Mama—I can't lie—I know you would agree with that. But I also want to make him happy. I just don't know how to do both."

four

In the days ahead, Sarah's preparations for a lonely evening meal became more common. Oftener than not, Papa came home late and ate a warmed-over supper by himself. Margaret now spent more time at Harriet's big white house on the bluff than she did at home. Barely seventeen, Harriet still considered herself one of the small town's socialites, so she drew Margaret into the very center of all the delightful activities the young girl had loved back home. Though Sarah didn't exactly approve of the gossiping, bold Harriet Anderson, she was pleased that Margaret had fit in so quickly. Of course, her sister had always possessed a talent for jumping into the hub of things.

A talent that I lack, she reflected honestly.

Margaret herself interrupted these reflections by exploding into the kitchen with her latest news. "Sarah, guess what? Harriet's having a party!" Sarah, who had been peacefully cutting bread for Papa's dinner, nearly sliced her finger at her sister's flurried entrance.

"So what's new? Harriet's always throwing parties," she replied testily. The near mishap made her feel irritated. Certainly this was not an earth-shaking announcement.

"But this one *will* be different! Some of the girls are going to do a little play. And there's going to be dancing!" Her eyes sparkled at the last word, and she gave a little clap. "It's going to be an adult party," she said, straightening up with new calm and attempting to look like a properly serious adult. "And I'm sure I will have to have an escort."

"Then you needn't begin looking for one, because you're not going. Sixteen is too young for an adult party with an escort."

"What?!" Margaret shrieked. "Why, Harriet's not much older than I am! There won't be anyone there I don't already know, I'm sure! They don't think I'm too young!"

"I'm not responsible for what Harriet and her friends are allowed to do. But you are too young."

Her sister's mouth opened and closed several times as she searched for an angry retort. "You're just jealous, Sarah, that's what it is. You're not invited to the parties. You just sit at home and. . .and bake bread," she finished, looking disdainfully at the knife and loaf her sister still held. "And you never have any friends because you never have any fun!" She stamped her foot. "Well, you're not going to spoil my fun. You're not responsible for me either, you know. You just think you are. I'll ask Papa. He'll say yes!" Margaret flung her final words as she spun out of the room, red-faced.

Sarah sighed, setting down her knife. It was true. She didn't have any authority to stop her sister. Only Papa did, and she knew Margaret was right, Papa would say yes. All she could do was offer sisterly advice, and any advice that conflicted with what her sister wanted to do wasn't likely to be heeded. A cold unease filled her heart at the thought of what this recklessness might mean for the girl's future.

Sarah's natural honesty forced her to consider Margaret's accusation. Was she jealous? She did wish she had the ease of making friends her sister had. Yet she wasn't sure she liked the sort of people Margaret's manner attracted. Nevertheless, Sarah hadn't made many friends in the time they had been there, and her often-solitary suppers only intensified the feelings of loneliness. "I do have friends at the church," she insisted, feeling a bit better. *But few your own age,* a small voice returned, and Sarah realized that most of her "friends" were older ladies, more mentors than friends.

The two older Winston girls, Ellen and Rachel, had welcomed her immediately. Ellen, only a year younger than

Sarah, shyly but enthusiastically offered her heart in friendship. Rachel, more reserved, as befitted her twenty-four years and position as pastor's wife, showed a calm acceptance Sarah admired. In some ways Rachel reminded Sarah of her older sister, Anne. She often found herself wanting to go to Rachel with her worries. But, she reasoned, the busy wife of a pastor mustn't always be troubled with her little anxieties. Besides, Rachel had other concerns right now, as she spent her evenings sewing clothes for a wee child who would need them when he or she arrived that winter.

"It's true, Lord," she said, conversing with God, as she often did when alone. "Not that I'm jealous, but I am lonely. I guess I've let myself believe I'm so busy here I just don't have time to socialize. But things are mostly cleaned up here, and goodness knows I needn't work away at suppers no one ever eats." She frowned at the knife she had resumed cutting with. "It's so much easier to just stay busy." *And safer too,* she suddenly realized. Her mother and Anne had been her two closest friends. She didn't want to risk anymore loss. "The fact is I'm really afraid to try.

"Well, that will change," she vowed, getting up to finish her task with new vigor. "I don't need to let my fears tell me what to do! I will make some real friends!" she said, slapping butter decisively on another slice of bread. Sarah looked down at her work. In her enthusiasm, she had prepared much more than they could possibly eat. She chuckled at herself. "Well, I guess Papa will get sandwiches for a few days. I hope he doesn't notice them getting a little old and dry!"

❧

On the appointed evening, a young man whose name Sarah didn't even know arrived to escort Margaret to the big party. Sarah's suggestion that Papa at least meet him before that night had also gone unheeded.

Papa had said yes to Margaret. Not only had he agreed to the party, but he had insisted she buy a new dress for the occasion.

Sarah knew better than to try to reason him out of the extravagance. She also knew they could ill afford the unnecessary expense. But now the big night was here, and Margaret was gone. She had looked lovely, Sarah admitted, if a little overdone. The green organdy dress she had chosen accented her newly pinned-up auburn hair and hazel eyes. *But she's so young for a dress and hairstyle so...so...grown up,* Sarah thought, surveying the girl. *Margaret is growing up,* she reminded herself. *But so quickly? Could this quick plunge into adult parties and entertainments be good for her? Or am I just making a big deal out of a girl's normal desire to be grown up and admired?* she wondered. Sarah shook her head, returning to the parlor chair and her mending.

"I really don't know, Lord," she uttered, looking at the ceiling. "You'll have to show me on this one. Show me what to do with this pretty, smart, hot-tempered child who isn't a child anymore. I really need your help." She didn't know how many times that evening she would have to remember that prayer.

❧

Six hours later, Sarah crossed the room yet again to peer out the window. No, Margaret hadn't appeared in the three or four minutes since she last performed that ritual. Rising panic and helplessness battled for control of her emotions as she stared into the darkness, chewing one knuckle.

"The party should have been over long ago," she said, breaking the tense silence. Sarah had noticed the signs of anxiety in her father too—the tapping finger as he sat pretending to read his accounts, the repeated trips to the coffeepot, the relieved start whenever they heard a noise outside, replaced by a worried look when the noise proved unfruitful. But neither had spoken of their shared concern.

She paced back to the table. "She should have been home long ago, Papa. I'll go crazy just sitting and waiting any longer. What should we do?"

Gerald Brown covered his eyes with his hands. "You haven't

been sitting, Sarah. You've been walking a hole in the floor, and it's about to make me crazy," he said, his voice rising. Papa sighed and looked up. "I'm sorry," he apologized, reaching for her hand. "We're both on edge."

"Ought we go down to the Anderson's and ask about her?"

"I'd been hoping we wouldn't need to do that—to let strangers know my daughter hasn't come home tonight. But I think it's about time. What will they think of us?"

Knowing Harriet Anderson's penchant for gossip, Sarah was afraid to imagine. No doubt the story, whatever it was, would be all over town tomorrow, once Harriet had been alerted. But right now fear for her sister's safety overrode concern for the family's reputation.

"I'll go down there now," Papa cut into her thoughts. "You go on to bed."

"No!" Sarah cried. "You can't think I could stay here and just go off to sleep, not knowing if she is safe! Oh, Papa, please let me come with you!"

Her father, who wasn't keen on the idea of both his daughters running around town past midnight, gave in when he saw the anxiety in her pleading eyes.

"All right, come. But don't you go off anywhere without me!" Within minutes, father and daughter drove off in the direction of the big white house on the bluff.

Papa's loud rap brought a confused-looking Mr. Anderson to the door. "Who is it? What's wrong?" he asked, trying to see the visitors through half-open eyes and darkness.

"Gerald Brown. I'm looking for my daughter. Is she still here?"

"Brown? Brown? Margaret's father? Here?" Carl Anderson began to waken completely. "Come in. Come in. You say she hasn't come home?" He squinted and shook his head to clear it. "But Harriet's party ended hours ago. No one's here," he said, waving a hand at the empty hallway as if to prove his words. "Sit down. Sit down. I'll go get Harriet to see if she knows what happened."

A very sleepy girl soon appeared at the bottom of the stairs. "Harriet, Mr. Brown and. . . ," he looked hesitantly at his other visitor.

"Sarah," she supplied. "Margaret's sister."

"Sarah," he finished, "are looking for Margaret. It seems she hasn't been home from your party. Did she say anything to you about where she might be going?"

"Margaret's not home yet?" Harriet asked, wide-eyed. "But she should have been. She was only. . . ." she broke off looking guilty.

"Only what?" prodded her father.

Harriet could see from the three sets of eyes staring at her that she had better tell the truth. "They went out on the river. In Harry's old boat. Harry and Bill wanted to show her the Piaza bird on the bluffs. She's new here. She's never seen it."

"The what?" asked Sarah.

"The Piaza bird," supplied Mr. Anderson. "The big mystery of Alton. It's a huge drawing high up on the walls of the river. No one knows how it got there. Makes it a curiosity to show to all newcomers."

"But to show them at this hour?" gasped Sarah. "Surely they couldn't expect to see much!"

"It doesn't sound like the sort of scheme they put much thought into all together," replied Harriet's father. "No telling what could have happened to them. A small dark boat on a huge river at night. . . ." He stopped, seeing the terror growing in Sarah's face. "At least we know what direction they went. I'm sure they're fine—probably just lost track of time. C'mon, we'll get the boys' fathers too and go looking."

Sarah jumped up from her chair, looking—rather than asking—to go along. Her mute plea didn't persuade her father this time.

"No, Sarah. Stay here for now. Scouring riverbanks isn't for young ladies. Stay and keep Miss Anderson company."

Frustrated, Sarah sat again. She knew he was right. She'd only impede the search. She would just have to wait. . .and wait.

&

In the end, she didn't have to wait long. The group of four men split up, and two of them came upon the very wet, tired trio, making their way back to town.

"We'll save the explanations—and the hollering—for later," Mr. Harris said, glaring at his son as soon as he realized all three had suffered no harm. He threw his dry coat around Margaret, and soon the entire group reassembled at the Anderson's. Hearing the commotion of the returning party, Sarah ran into the yard.

"Oh, Margaret," she cried, pulling her sister into a relieved hug.

"I'm all wet. . .and dirty," the girl protested.

"So you are," she laughed. "So you are. Come in and get warmed." She forgot anger in her happiness at seeing Margaret whole and alive.

"And just look at my dress!"

Sarah did look. The once-lovely green dress now stuck to her sister's legs in muddy, wet folds. Burrs clung to its hem, and a small tear pulled at the waist. *Salvageable,* Sarah thought, *but that new, expensive dress will never look the same.*

"It doesn't matter right now." She hustled Margaret into the warm house. "But where have you been?"

The story unfolded as three chattering young people stood by the newly stoked fire in the Anderson kitchen.

"Well, we never made it to see the bird," began a sheepish Harry. "Didn't bring enough oil for the lantern. . . ."

"Didn't bring enough common sense for any of ye," muttered his father.

Harry blushed. "So. . .so it went out, the light I mean, and everything was dark and. . .and well, it's a big river to steer a boat on in the dark."

Sarah's eyes widened at the thought of what might have happened. *A wrong turn, a strong current, another larger boat . . . .* She shivered, suddenly feeling as cold as they looked.

"We hit a sandbar," continued Bill. "Hit it hard. And we couldn't get off. Almost got thrown out with the impact, all three of us." Looking at the frightened, angry faces around him, he realized this was a detail he should have omitted. "Uh . . .but we weren't too far out. We could walk ashore. That is, we could," he looked at Harry. "Margaret—Miss Brown, I mean— she rode on my shoulders. But it was a long walk home, through woods and grasses and such. And dark—kinda hard to see the way, even when you know where you're goin'."

"Which we didn't," added Harry, not noticing his friend's glare.

"Found 'em a half mile or so outside o' town, goin' in circles. Goin' in circles. Just what one might expect!" spat one of the men. He turned toward his son. "And if you think, boy, we're going to forget this adventure. . . ."

The other boy's father broke in. "It's been a long night— we're all tired and wet. Maybe it's best if we go home, get some rest, and take care of this in the morning, when tempers aren't quite so short." His look at his own son promised a reckoning soon. "Let poor Anderson have his house back."

"Yes, let's get home before you catch a chill," said Sarah, bundling her sister in a borrowed blanket.

Margaret broke the silence as they drove home. "Well, honestly," she complained, "I'll never trust those boys again when they say something is supposed to be fun!"

five

"You see, I'm new here. Arrived just now actually." Sarah overheard the flustered young woman speaking to the man at the counter. Sarah had come down to her father's river warehouse to bring him his forgotten dinner and wandered into that area's general store on a whim. Now her attention was caught by someone apparently newer to town than even Sarah herself.

"And I don't know where I'm going," continued the unknown person. "I. . .I'm here to teach school, but I need to locate the place. . . ."

"Don't got no school here. Don't need none," the man behind the counter replied gruffly. Sarah smiled at the irony of his very ungrammatical declaration.

"No, no, wait," the girl called at the already retreating storekeeper. "You don't have one because I'm supposed to start it. It's not a public school. It's a mission school. With a church here. I need to find a Reverend. . . ," she searched her bag and pulled out a worn letter. "A Reverend Josiah Meyers."

Sarah was startled to hear the name of her own pastor.

"Well, I don't know much 'bout church stuff. Don't know where ye might find him. And we still don't need no school." This time he did leave her, to offer help to his other customers.

"Well, I thank you for that fine welcome to your town," Sarah heard the girl mutter under her breath.

"Perhaps I can do better," she offered with a smile. "I haven't been here long either, but I do know where to find my own pastor's home."

"Reverend Meyers? Oh, really? Could you direct me? I'm so hot and tired from the long trip. I just need to settle in."

"Of course. Our buggy is outside. Come—I'll take you there."

31

"Oh, that would be wonderful!" her new acquaintance cried with relief. "I know I should tell you please don't go to the bother, but I can't. I'm just so grateful to avoid the walk!"

"I know what it is to be new here. We moved from Washington only six weeks ago. I'm still finding my way around." Sarah helped place the woman's baggage in her buggy.

"I'm Hannah," said the young woman, offering her hand. "Hannah Woods. I've just come from Cincinnati. That's not as far as Washington, so I guess I'm not quite as displaced as you, though I sure feel it right now." She climbed up to her seat with a laugh.

"Sarah Brown. I'm sure you'll feel at home soon. Not everyone is as gruff as our store friend," she laughed. "In fact, you'll find Pastor Meyers and his wife are wonderful people."

"I'm sure I will. We've corresponded a bit, of course. I suppose if it's your church you know all about the school plans."

"No, I don't. I was surprised to hear you speak of it. I've heard nothing at all." Sarah flipped the reins over her horses.

"Perhaps that's because plans weren't final until very recently. Everything had to be checked and rechecked, and my application approved, and I. . .had to be certain I wanted to come." Sarah noticed Hannah's eyes misted slightly. "That it was the Lord's will I come," she finished with more certainty and a lift of her chin. "And it was, so here I am!" Behind her bright tone there was still a hint of sadness. Unwilling to pry, Sarah mentally filed her impression, hoping to learn more later.

"I expect, it being nearly September now, I'll be starting soon. I'm a bit nervous. I've taught before, but not like this. City schools are much different than one-room mission schools, but I don't need to tell you that, do I? You're from the city. And if that 'gentleman,' " she laid heavy emphasis on the word, "is representative of people's opinions, it may be difficult to get students. What if no one really does want a school?"

"I'm sure he's not representative. Probably just an old water-front bachelor—crusty and suspicious. Reverend Meyers wouldn't have asked you if he didn't believe folks would come. But. . .our church is small. . .I can't imagine we could afford to run a school."

"Well you're not, alone. We have a large church back in Cincinnati. They're supplying the books and equipment and such. And me," she added with a smile. "The church here provides the building and my own room and board."

"I don't quite understand though. I guess I thought there were public schools everywhere. Papa sent us to private schools but. . .I just supposed everyone had a place to go to school."

"Illinois has set up the system. They've set aside the land for schools. But that's as far as they've gotten. I don't know how much longer it will take. In the meantime, it's a wonderful opportunity for the church."

"Speaking of the church. . .here we are. This is it, and Pastor Meyers' home is right through the trees." Sarah hesitated. "If. . .if you find you need some things after settling in. . .I'd be happy to take you to the store—not the one we were just in," she amended, laughing. Sarah was shy to press a friendship with this stranger. Yet hadn't she asked God for a friend? And this one had practically been set right in front of her. Besides, something in Hannah intrigued and attracted her. Perhaps it was the woman's certainty—her calm assurance of being in the Lord's will in the midst of a strange place and strange people. Sarah wished she had that certainty.

"I'd like that," said Hannah. "Maybe sometime next week . . . ."

"How about Monday morning? You'll have seen your home and school, and will have been to the church—you'll probably be just ready to dig in to keeping house."

"Wonderful. I'll have my list and be waiting for you. Thank you, Sarah. I'm so glad we met—I did feel awfully alone in that store. Now that I have one friend, I feel I can face this new town and anything it has for me!"

Sarah smiled. "I'm glad. I'm still not sure even I can say that! I'll see you Sunday, I suppose. Good luck."

❧

On Monday, Sarah brought Hannah to Green's store, the same

place she had passed that first Saturday. Mrs. O'Reilly, she knew, wasn't exactly the picture of amiability, but she was better than the man at the riverfront, and the store was close.

"Yer new here, ain't ya?" asked Liza O'Reilly, as Hannah handed her her list of necessities.

"Yes, ma'am. I just came on Friday. I'm here to start a school. Do you have any children of the right age?"

"School, eh? No, don't got no young'uns of my own, but I guess as it wouldn't hurt others. Lessee—we can start with the washtub and put all yer things into it. Soap, sugar, eggs—no, guess I'd better put them on top, huh? From back East you say? Like this 'un?" She jabbed her bony finger toward Sarah.

"Ohio, ma'am. Cincinnati."

"Oh. Wal, just be sure ye stick to school teachin'. We here know why it is young girls come out from the East. All the same. Ye say it's for one reason—school teachin', churchin', whatever." She shot a reproachful glare that encompassed both girls. "But girls come west to git 'em husbands, and that's the long 'n short of it. More plentiful here than where you come from, I s'pose. No, we don't take too kindly to pretty young things comin' here and stealin' our good menfolk." Once more she glared at Sarah, who wasn't sure how to defend herself against accusations that had never entered her head. She certainly hadn't chosen to come here, after all!

"Actually," Hannah calmly replied, "I am already engaged. My fiancé is attending college back home, and I am gaining experience until he finishes. So you see, I'd be happy to stay away from your good menfolk, and I'm sure you would be happy to tell them all so. Now, how much do I owe you?" she asked.

Sarah turned away to smother a laugh. Hannah had figured the good shopkeeper correctly. A gossip she definitely was, and the new schoolteacher's ineligibility would be old news before long. Yet Hannah had put her in her place so smoothly, Sarah wasn't even sure the woman realized it.

six

A warm breeze played with blond and brown hair as two young women watched a steamboat ply the river waters below them. Sarah and Hannah sat on top of one of Alton's tallest hills with a spur-of-the-moment picnic spread before them. In the two weeks since they had met, the two had become fast friends.

"I wish I could go with them," said Sarah, gazing after the retreating boat. "I wish I could steam up and down the river and find something new at every turn."

"Truly? I wouldn't think it of you. You don't seem quite the adventurous type."

Sarah smiled and looked down. "No, you're right there. I'm sure if I ever got the chance I'd be much too scared to really do it. Not like you," she sighed.

"Like me?"

"You came hundreds of miles to a strange place—alone—and started a school you didn't even know anyone would come to. That's adventurous."

Hannah shrugged. "I don't know. It's what seemed the right thing to do. I didn't think about it as an adventure—although I was frightened. Sometimes God just sets these kinds of opportunities in front of you and says, 'Here's a chance to grow. What are you going to do with it?' And I almost didn't take it."

"Well, I'm not seeing any of those opportunities in front of me. No, I don't think I'm really adventurous at all, just. . . ."

"Bored?" Hannah offered.

"Yes," she laughed. "I think that may be it. Silly, isn't it? A whole new town, new friends to make, places to explore, a new home to keep in order. And in the middle of it all, I'm bored."

She played with the piece of raspberry cake before her.

"I don't think it's silly. Sometimes big changes like that only seem to point out that, well, that your life is still the same. That all your surroundings have changed but you still feel like the same old person."

"Yes! Exactly! You know, in the beginning, it felt kind of exciting to run Papa's house—to take care of them and be in charge and know they needed me. And I still want to do that. But. . .do I want to do it for the rest of my life? At seventeen I didn't think about things like that. But now. . .now I'm twenty years old, and I don't even know what I want to do. Or what I can do."

"What do you think you want?"

"I'm not sure. I just know I need to feel a purpose. Like you. You're teaching. You're going to be a missionary. How did you decide that? How did you know God wanted you to take those steps?"

"Sarah, I didn't come here because I felt an inescapable call of God. I came because I could do the work. I was trained as a teacher. I saw the opportunity as a way to use the training and gifts God gave me."

"But how could you be sure then?"

Hannah thought a moment. "Does He ever promise absolute certainty? I don't know. I think God's will is something that happens to us while we're trying to do right. A lot of folks pass up a lot of chances to be what God wants because they're sitting around waiting for something to hit them on the head. Sure, there are people who feel a definite call to be missionaries or preachers or whatever. That's wonderful. But for most of us? Maybe who we are is more important that what we do."

"That's easy for you to say. You have some training and abilities. I don't. But I so desperately want to do something that matters."

"If that's truly what you want, Sarah, He'll certainly show you where you belong. God's not in the habit of turning down willing servants."

"I know, just be patient." She groaned and then began laughing.

"Well, Papa isn't going to be patient about his supper if I don't get on my way home. We've dawdled away a lot of time!" She folded up their picnic blanket and scattered the crumbs for the birds. Hannah straightened as well, looking thoughtful.

"Hm. Sarah, do you know anything about music?"

"Yes, I had piano lessons back home. And I've sung quite a bit."

Hannah nodded. "I thought I remembered Pastor Meyers saying you have a beautiful voice."

Sarah blushed.

"Would you be interested. . .willing. . . . You see, I'm supposed to teach these children music. But I've been afraid to start because I know how awful I am at it. Would you like to do it? It would only be an hour or so, once or twice a week. Not much, but it's something to start with, if you're really looking for opportunities. Of course, they couldn't pay you . . . ."

"I?" Sarah broke in. "Do you think I could? I don't know anything about teaching."

"But you know music, and I don't. You might teach them to sing hymns and things. Nothing too complicated. Oh, you could do it, I'm sure!"

Sarah's face glowed with excitement. Maybe she could. She pictured herself in a room full of children, singing the hymns she loved so well. It wasn't earth-shaking, but maybe, maybe this was where she belonged.

"I'd love to try. I really would. I'll talk to Papa about it tonight. As soon as I can."

She hurried home, her head whirling with plans for bringing music to the children at the little mission school. How much did they know? Where should she start? Was there music available? How could she make it interesting to all ages? New ideas replaced others scarcely formulated as she considered all the possibilities. She could barely contain her excitement until that evening, when Papa would be relaxing at home.

❧

"Papa, I visited Hannah today. . . . We went on a picnic." Sarah set the cup of coffee she brought him down on the parlor table.

"Um. Nice girl," he said from behind his paper. "That's the one here to do some teaching, right?"

"Yes. Well, I was telling her how, since we're all settled here now and everything, how I wished for some other activity to fill time."

"We don't keep you busy enough around here? Then you've got to be more social. Margaret doesn't have any trouble finding things to do. Always flying about here and there. I'm not even sure where she is now." He furrowed his forehead with the sudden realization. "Hopefully, not out on the river," he muttered under his breath. "You've just got to get out and make friends."

"Yes, Papa, but I don't mean just filling my time. I mean doing something that—that means something." She groped for words that wouldn't belittle her sister's activities. "Something that makes me feel important." She hesitated. "Hannah mentioned that the children need a music teacher. She doesn't feel confident doing it herself. And well, with my training, she thought perhaps I could do it. . . ."

"My daughters do not teach!" he shouted, throwing down the paper. His vehemence startled her. "They stay at home like proper young ladies!"

"But Papa, it wouldn't really be like teaching. More like . . .like charity work. Only an hour or two a week of volunteering my time. . . ."

"It's the same thing to me! Next you'll be wanting to start your own school for farmer's children. If you want to do charity work, sew quilts and bandages! No daughter of mine is going to have to work!"

Sarah stood with her mouth open, too shocked to reply. She had not expected such violent opposition to what she thought a small task.

"Yes, Papa," she finally managed. She moved quietly to

escape from the room, her throat tight with disappointment. Alone upstairs, she sank onto the bed, still subdued with shock. *He said no!* It would be useless, she knew, to try again. On this point he was clearly adamant. But why? And she had been so sure! All the happy plans she'd made for ministering to the children taunted her.

"Lord," she cried out. "I'm so confused!" She began to pace across the room. "I thought You had a place for me! I thought this was Your plan, that You were leading me. Why? Why did You close the door? I don't understand!" She pounded frustrated fists on the windowsill. "Please," she begged, sinking to her knees, "please help me understand." She knelt at the window, looking out as if an answer would come from the wind rustling her back-yard trees.

The answer did come. Softly into her memory the words familiar filtered—words her mother had often quoted. "For I know the thoughts which I think toward you. . . ." Where was that from? *Yes, Jeremiah,* she remembered, going to retrieve her worn Bible from its place on her desk.

If anyone ever had cause to be confused about his calling, she thought, it was the prophet Jeremiah. The Lord called him to preach a mighty message of repentance, yet no one ever listened. He could easily have wondered if the Lord was still leading him—wondered why doors seemed to close. She found the quotation in chapter 29, verse 11. "Thoughts of peace, and not of evil, to give you a future and a hope." Yet here Jeremiah was, assuring these same people who had tortured him that the Lord had forgotten none of them, that He had a plan. He would not abandon them.

"And You won't abandon me either, will You, Lord?" She knelt again at the windowsill. "Thank you," she prayed. "I know You have a hope and a future for me too. Forgive me for not trusting You. If teaching wasn't Your idea, I don't want to do it. I know You have something better for me."

Sarah remained at the window a few moments. Peace began to wash over her confused feelings. The sadness of her unused plans ebbed away while she remained still. She would go tell Hannah tomorrow.

&

Hannah was not alone when Sarah called. Harriet Anderson sat in the small room, merrily spouting the latest gossip, oblivious to her hostess' nonresponsiveness.

"And I'm just determined to be married before I'm eighteen," she chattered. "Not like that Katherine Brewster. Mrs. Kendall told me she's turned down another offer. Just who does she think she is? She's not getting any younger you know—almost twenty-two! Soon the men won't be coming around anymore, and then she'll be sorry."

Sarah and Hannah, both twenty themselves, showed no appreciation for this remark.

"If Katherine hasn't met a man she loves, she should turn them down," said Hannah quietly.

"What about you?" Harriet asked. "Any word when your wedding is to be?"

"William will be finished with his schooling in two years. We plan to marry then."

"Two years! What a long wait! I could never be apart so long! Why didn't you stay with him? What if he finds another girl?"

"Then I would know it's not God's will we be together," she answered simply. She refused to explain her reasons for delay to one of the town gossips.

Sarah already knew the answers to Harriet's questions. It would not be practical for them to marry while William remained in school. They had considered the opportunity to teach in a mission school a chance for Hannah to gain some experience that would prove useful when they became missionaries overseas—even if it meant a painful separation. She knew, too, that her friend's apparent unconcern didn't stem from a lack of love for William. Hardly a day passed without letters exchanged between the betrothed couple, and more than once Sarah had seen the evidence of tears when her friend had been thinking about her loved one so far away.

"Did you come for something in particular, Sarah?" Hannah turned the conversation. "Did you ask your father?"

"Yes," she said, her face showing her disappointment as she sat down near the two girls. "I'm afraid he said no. He doesn't feel it would be. . . ," she searched for a neutral word, "appropriate."

Harriet looked interested. "What's this? What's not appropriate?"

Sarah sighed. "Hannah asked if I could teach music to her pupils. It sounded like something I would like very much, but. . . Papa said no and I must abide by that."

"Well I wouldn't! Not if it was something I really wanted to do. I'm old enough to do what I like, and I'd just tell him so!"

"It's not that easy," Hannah interjected.

"Why not?"

"For one thing, the Bible says we must obey our parents," Sarah explained.

"Fiddlesticks! That's just for little kids."

"I believe it's for as long as I'm under his roof and his care. Unless, of course, he wants me to do something wrong," she added, remembering his wish that she lie about their wealth.

"Well, it wouldn't take me long to get out from under his roof then." Harriet tossed her head. "I'd get married."

"Rather a drastic solution, I would think," Hannah observed. "Especially since then we must obey our husbands."

Harriet wrinkled her nose. "Anyway, everyone says how you just devote yourself to making that man happy, and then he just turns around and says you can't do something for yourself. I don't know why you bother. I wouldn't."

"I wish everyone," Sarah emphasized the word, "would refrain from discussing my family. I must be going, Hannah. I'm very sorry about the class. I hope you can work something out."

"They'll just have to suffer along with me, I guess. We can at least make a joyful noise to the Lord—even if noise is all I can manage!"

"You'll do fine. And it'll be good experience for all the things missionaries are called on for that they have no idea how to do," Sarah laughed.

Alone on the road, their conversation nagged at her. She felt angry, mainly because Harriet's comments reflected feelings she herself had spent much time trying to conquer. She was an adult. She should be able to do as she wished. And it certainly wasn't fair. Old resentments she thought she had stifled rose again. Why did she bother?

Once more, Sarah reviewed in her mind her mother's last message to her. Mama had been converted in the revivals that swept the country under Charles Finney. Her oldest two girls had listened well to her teaching and accepted Jesus as their Saviour. But nine years of prayer and living as a godly wife had made no change in Papa's resistance to what he called her "emotional time of life." As Amelia Brown lay dying, her final sorrow had not been for herself, but for her husband. Sarah could not forget her words.

"It's up to you now, Sarah. Anne will be going her own way soon, leaving home. You're the strong one. Your father's soul is always in the Lord's keeping, I know, but I'm leaving it to your earthly care. Promise me you'll do your best to see that he joins me in heaven."

Frightened and dazed, sixteen-year-old Sarah had pledged herself to the task of an adult. Many times she had resented that pledge. She didn't feel strong. Often she cried in frustrated loneliness, "Lord, I can't! Why is this my burden? I'm too young to care for me, let alone him!" But she was twenty now, and it was her charge to keep. Yes, as her mother had said, no one could be responsible for Papa except the Lord. Yet Sarah knew she would work with Him for as long as it took. No one had promised it would be easy. But she loved him, and he needed her. And the Lord would help, as He always had. "I have a plan," she repeated to herself. "A plan for a hope and a future." She began to step more lightly as she continued on her way.

seven

"Sarah—you'll never guess who was here while you were gone!" Margaret greeted her at the door, unable to wait for her to get all the way inside.

"President Fillmore," Sarah responded playfully. "And he's coming to dinner Sunday, right?" She continued past her sister to set her bonnet down on the hallway table.

"He's got more sense than to leave civilization and come out here." Margaret's tone indicated she wished her father had had such sense. "No. Almost as good. Mrs. Winston and her daughter Ellen. What do you think? She invited us to dinner Saturday night. All of us! You know, Harriet says they're the richest family in town. And I've never been there. You have. And it's not fair too," she gave a little stamp. "What's it like? Is it as nice as our house was?"

"How can I answer all your questions if you don't take a break in between?" Sarah laughed. She thought a moment. "Well, no, it's not. . .not at all like our old house. I don't think . . .well, you can't really compare them." How could she explain the difference to her sister—especially a difference she herself only half understood? Papa's wealth had been so obvious—part of the show he always enjoyed. But there. . . . "Yes, it's a large home," she finally answered, "but you won't find the carpets and fancy papers and hangings and such. They're just not that kind of people."

"But wasn't Harriet right? Aren't they that rich?"

"I. . .I suppose. That's what people say anyway." Sarah felt uneasy with the conversation.

"Then what does he do with all of it?"

"I don't know. It's not something I intend to ask, Margaret. It's

43

no one's business but their own." She picked up a *Godey's* magazine, attempting to end the conversation.

"Of course I wouldn't ask," Margaret huffed, "but I can be curious." She turned out of the parlor, leaving Sarah to her magazine and her thoughts.

As Sarah skimmed through the pages of home decorations and fancy gowns, Margaret's questions nagged at her. What did Mr. Winston do with all of his money? Of course, there was the church, but it couldn't be the only beneficiary. Yet while everyone knew who endowed the local charities, his name had not been coupled with any that she had heard. She pulled her eyebrows together in thought. "Oh, dear, now I'm doing just what I scolded her for: speculating on someone else's business."

Margaret poked her head back in the door. "What should I wear?"

"I think your green dress would be more than adequate. I've mended it, and it looks almost new again," Sarah answered.

"I don't see how it could, after that awful night," answered Margaret, wrinkling her nose. "I'll probably always smell dirty river water now whenever I wear it."

"I don't suppose I need tell you who's to blame for that," reproved her sister, tossing down the magazine and standing up. "I guess I'd better get to the baking. But who wants to cook in this weather? I wonder when fall comes around here."

❧

Saturday came—though not soon enough for the impatient Margaret. When all were counted, eleven people sat around the Winston dining table—their family of six; Rachel's husband, Pastor Meyers; Hannah; and Sarah's family. Margaret found kind listeners in Ellen Winston and her younger sister, fifteen-year-old Joanna. The two girls rarely got in much to say themselves, but that seemed to suit all three. Their end of the table was filled with bright chatter.

Conversation at the other end took a different note.

"Hear about those two men got caught across the river trying to steal slaves?" asked Mr. Brown. He stabbed the air with his fork in indignant emphasis. "Don't know what they'll get, but it should be a lesson, I think."

Mr. Winston glanced at his son. "Yes, we've heard. It's hard to say what will happen to them. There were three men some years back up in Quincy who got twelve years in a Missouri jail for it. And most folks thought that was lucky. The crowds had already built a scaffold to hang them on. I expect they felt a little cheated it didn't get used after all."

"For what?" Sarah asked. "What exactly did they do to deserve that?"

"Missouri authorities set up some slaves as decoys, acting as if they wanted information on how to escape to Canada and freedom. But when the three men tried to give it to them, they were arrested instead."

Papa nodded with satisfaction. "Just as it should be."

"I don't understand. I thought Papa said they stole slaves. . . ."

"Same thing," Mr. Brown interjected. "Tellin' them how to get away from those that rightly own 'em is stealing to me."

"It's stealing as far as the law's concerned too," added Mr. Winston. "The climate over there in Quincy might be even worse now," he continued. "They might even be hanged. It's hard to say."

"Would serve those wild abolitionists well if they were," Papa answered. "Always trying to tell folks they know what's right. Trying to push their moral ideas on me and others. Doing nothing but causing trouble, I think. We had 'em all over Washington too. Coming down from Massachusetts and making their noise. Slavery's legal and that's that. And we're all better off for it." He paused, waiting for agreement. Sarah stared at her plate, while the others looked around at each other. No one seemed willing to comment on his philosophy.

"And I hear," he said leaning forward with his most disgusted tone, "they've even got women doing their preaching and lecturing these days!" He sat back, with a look that clearly showed what he thought of such dangerous strategies.

"It's been my experience," said Pastor Meyers, looking affectionately at his wife, "that in matters of practical morality, women often do have greater sense."

"Well, it's unseemly, that's what it is. I wish I were a younger man. I'd be willing to collect those big rewards for runaways before any do-gooders made off with them."

"Papa!" cried Sarah. "Surely you wouldn't—no matter what you think of abolitionists!"

"Surely I would, dear girl. A man can use all the extra money he can get. Not, of course," he added looking at George Winston, "that we need it. But one must be sensible."

Sarah sat back in shocked silence. She wasn't certain herself what she thought of all the aspects of the slavery question. But the thought of capturing a man who had risked his life for freedom and selling him back into bondage—how could any money repay one for that ransom of his soul? Even in Washington, where slavery was legal, slave catchers had been looked upon as necessary evils—people to do business with but not to mingle with socially. She couldn't believe her own father would do such a horrible thing.

"I just like to stay clear of the whole mess," said Mr. Winston. "Safest that way. Make no enemies on either side. Then when questions start being asked, you know nothing and can sleep easy. Marvelous turkey, Charlotte. I suppose I should let the guests say so first, but I have to tell the truth. Can't wait for dessert."

"You won't have to wait if the girls will give me some help in the kitchen," she answered, looking at the other end of the table.

"Let me help," Sarah jumped up.

"No, dear, you just sit at the table and be waited on yourself for a change. We can take care of it." She ushered her two youngest children toward the door. The bread pudding and coffee they bore back to the table a few minutes later confirmed Mr. Winston's hopes. No one talked while they savored the delicious dish, and by the time Charlotte Winston suggested some parlor games and music, all hazardous conversation seemed to be forgotten.

Soon the young people sat around the board to "Mansion of Happiness," preparing to play. "Come join us, Mother," urged Rachel. Mrs. Winston hovered undecidedly between her husband and the livelier group. "They're going to talk business." Her daughter tilted her head toward the two men, already in close conference at the other end of the room. "You'd much rather be with us, and you know it."

Mrs. Winston easily gave up the battle with her inclination. "All right, I will play. But you'll have to tell me how, because this is brand new to me."

Margaret, Ellen, and Joanna kept up their supper-time enthusiasm. Rachel and Charlotte smiled with more restrained delight at the points they won. David alone seemed immune to the contagious gaiety. He played only half aware of what he was doing. Only once did he brighten up to his usual self, but then the curtain came quickly down again over his face, and Sarah felt especially excluded from his attention the rest of the evening.

I'm just being overly sensitive, she told herself more than once. *It's not me in particular. He's cold to everyone.* But she couldn't exactly say why the fact that this wasn't true hurt so much.

In the opposite corner, the two men were indeed deep in conversation about business concerns. "Got to work extra hard to build up the line to Chicago," Mr. Brown was saying, "before winter comes and any shipping there is over."

"Ever thought of railroads?" asked Mr. Winston. "They're still pretty new here in Illinois, but very promising. Investment in the Chicago-Alton might be a good idea right now."

"That so? Something to think about. A man could make a lot of money out here if he wanted to. A lot of money."

"Ah, but what does it prosper a man to gain the whole world and lose his soul? Ever look at what the Bible has to say there, Gerald?"

"The Bible? Oh, I suppose I must have once or twice. Can't really remember. No time for that sort of thing, you know. I'm a busy man."

"But what a shame it would be if on that last day the Lord had to say He had no time for you." He shook his head. "He'll never say it 'til you make Him say it by never choosing to follow Him in this life. But if you never make time for Him. . . I don't want to see you regretting it, my friend."

Mr. Brown shifted uncomfortably. "Yes, well, sometime, sometime. Maybe I'll just come to that church with Sarah someday. Maybe I will. But tell me more of the railroad. . . ."

Margaret, as Sarah expected, won the game. Her sister had a knack for games that made her hard to beat, even if she had never played before. Sarah, however, outshone the rest around the piano later. Several times the others dropped out to listen to her clear tones singing her favorite hymns. To her great amazement, her father even asked her to sing more as they made their way home later.

eight

The next morning promised a clear, late-summer sky for the picnic that was to follow church. Sarah rose early to prepare the fresh cornbread and blackberry jam she planned to bring as her contribution. She was excited that she had persuaded Margaret to come. A deepening friendship with Joanna and Ellen Winston would be no bad thing for her sister, she thought. It might balance at least the wilder sorts of friends she always had around. *The kind,* Sarah still shook her head at the thought, *who took young girls on midnight boat trips.* She could smile about it now, but it had taken some time to develop a sense of humor about the incident.

Walking out to the nearby hill after church, Sarah saw her sister striding in her direction. Margaret joined her as the ladies began setting up the food in a line, but she did not long need Sarah's help in meeting people. Soon she had found the other girls her age and was off into a rousing game of shuttlecock before Sarah knew she had left her side.

Several women who lived close by arrived with the hot dishes they had returned home to get. They shooed Sarah and the other younger girls away, finishing the food preparation themselves.

"Go, go on. You've done your part. We'll take over. You go an' have some fun now. I'm used to gettin' a meal ready for a group this size," grinned Mrs. Dougherty, moving in to take her place. Sarah laughed, knowing this mother of twelve children—and ten of them boys—could indeed manage a much larger task than a mere church picnic. She moved off to watch the footraces the men and boys had organized, linking arms with

Hannah as they walked.

"Sarah, Hannah—just in time. We need some pretty ladies to hand out ribbons to the victors." Sarah hardly recognized the Pastor Meyers who now hailed them to hurry over. With his shirtsleeves rolled up and his Sunday coat discarded over a tree branch, he no longer appeared the serious preacher she knew from the pulpit.

"Would I be thought of as doing a ministry for the church then, sir?" she asked in mock seriousness.

"Of course—Paul does speak of running the race to receive a prize, you know."

"Then I suppose we may consider this our calling, Hannah, at least for today," she added, her eyes dancing with fun. The beauty of the day made laughter contagious.

"I winned, I winned, Miss Sarah! Did you see? Did you see?!" A beaming Johnnie Dougherty ran to her side to receive his blue ribbon.

"I did. I'll bet you can outrun all nine of your brothers!"

Johnnie blushed. "Naw. They've got such long legs, y' know. But I'm gonna catch up someday!" He ran off to show his ribbon to everyone he could find.

The next boy—older and more conscious of what the other fellows thought—wanted nothing to do with the praise of "girls," no matter what age. "Thanks," he mumbled, and slipped away from her as quickly as he could.

"We won, fair and square!" a girl's voice hollered. Sarah looked up in surprise to see Margaret, laughing and windblown, coming for her victor's ribbon.

"No, you didn't. We just slowed down to let you," yelled two boys her age. "Wouldn't be polite t' beat girls!"

Margaret just laughed again, along with her companion, who was still tied to her at the ankles. "What do you think, Sarah?" she asked. "I got Louise to run with me, and we beat all those boys!" She threw a haughty look at the second-place finishers on the word *all*. "But I guess you'd say I was most unladylike."

Margaret straightened and held her hand out for her ribbon, with an air that said she didn't really care what Sarah thought.

Her sister laughed. "Maybe. But you did win, didn't you?" She hugged Margaret and handed her the prize. Sarah looked toward the sky. "As long as she can still do things like that, Lord, I guess I needn't be afraid she's quite ready to grow up completely. Thank You for just a little more time."

The various races continued, and Sarah smiled, especially to pin a winning ribbon on David in the men's long race.

"Is that all he gets?" joked another finisher nearby.

Sarah blushed and turned away to Hannah. Why did people always have to get other ideas when a man and woman were just friends? She couldn't imagine what could lead anyone to believe otherwise. *Especially today,* she thought, with a sudden dropping of spirits. Paying no attention to the remark, David turned away to get some lemonade with another girl. Clearly, last night's mood hadn't passed. He still held something against her.

Races done, the women called everyone over to enjoy the outdoor dinner they had so lavishly displayed. Sarah didn't think she was particularly hungry, but the smells of roast beef, ham, various breads and pies, and fresh fruits aroused an appetite that could do justice to all their hard work.

"Everything always tastes better outdoors," she told Hannah, leaning back against a tree. "But now I think I'd better follow Margaret's example and run a few races or I'll have to unlace two inches at least!" She folded her hands with exaggerated difficulty over her stomach.

"I can't promise a race, but how about a walk?" Sarah jumped at David's unexpected voice behind her, then blushed when she realized he must have heard her speak of lacing. She looked at him in confusion. A half hour ago he hadn't even wanted to speak to her and now. . . . She shrugged her shoulders.

"All right, that will have to do, since, unlike my sister, I'm regrettably past the age when running is acceptable." She smiled and offered her hand to be helped to her feet. They strolled together up the bluff to look out over the distant river below. He still seemed remote—as cold and detached as he had the night before. Sarah missed the air of warm friendship she had felt developing, but she wasn't sure how to break the silence.

"It's a beautiful river," she offered at last. "I sometimes imagine going from where it begins all the way down to New Orleans. What an adventure that would be! And right across there, an entirely different state. Imagine!"

"Yes, a very different state."

"Missouri? Why do you say that?"

"Because it's the South and we're the North. Though parts of Illinois aren't too sure about that. And one day, I think that river may divide these two states in the greatest difference this country has ever known." He spoke sadly, almost as if she were no longer there. Silence hung again.

"You mean slavery. But why do you say parts of this state aren't sure? You said that before—that Illinois isn't as free as I thought. Why? I can see abolitionist thought being dangerous over there," she waved her hand toward the opposite bank, "but why here?"

"Abolitionist sentiment is common here in Alton, but not popular. Ever heard of Elijah Lovejoy?"

"Of course. Murdered here simply because he believed in freedom of the press."

"His press was abolitionist. People across the river didn't look kindly on his *Observer*. Chased him out of St. Louis, and folks here decided to finish the job. Tried to burn him and his press to the ground. But they shot him before the building burned. Of course, I wasn't very old then, but I remember. Seems some people only believe in freedom of the press when it's their opinion that's free."

"But I still don't see why people here didn't share his opinions."

"You've got to remember where the settlers here came from. They're Southerners at heart, from Virginia and the Carolinas.

Kentucky too. All good slave states. They didn't own slaves themselves and so couldn't survive in that economy. Most chose the unknown evil of the western frontier over the known evil of starvation."

"I'd think they'd hate slavery then, if it was the cause of their poverty."

"Some do. But others. . . . They may not have liked slavery because of what it did to them, but they hated the colored man more. Human nature takes all kinds of strange quirks, doesn't it?

"And Illinois actually has a lot of slave labor," he continued. "They hire slaves from masters in Kentucky and Missouri. They're not Illinois slaves, because they're paid. But they're someone's slaves, and no one here seems to be too concerned about that detail."

Sarah listened thoughtfully. She'd never heard him come so close to an abolitionist speech. Up until now, she hadn't been able to determine his beliefs on the subject, but surely a Christian man must feel as she did. But then, there were many Christian men in the South too.

"I see. Mama taught us it was so simple. Man is made in God's image, no matter how young or old, smart or foolish, or what color he is. So one person must never take away the dignity of another. But it's not that easy is it? There are a lot of questions mixed up in the issue—questions I don't know the answers to."

"What answers do you know, Sarah? Obviously, your mother's feelings didn't apply to the entire household."

"What? Oh, you mean what Papa said last night. It's not the first issue Papa and I haven't exactly agreed upon. Certainly I agree with Mama that a person ought never. . .well, ought never do to another what he wouldn't have done to him. And a person's a person, no matter what he looks like. That's the most ridiculous thing I can imagine, to say someone isn't human when he can't possibly be anything else. But I can't help but be uneasy about some of the things abolitionists do. Surely even for a

good goal it's not right to do wrong. Take Mr. Garrison, for example. It seems he's doing more harm than the problem he wants
to alleviate with all his talk of just scrapping the Union."

"Ah, and he also advocates the great sin your father railed
against. He allows—no encourages—women to lecture. What's
your opinion there? Do you believe the Grimke sisters should
be silenced, as so many others do?"

"It was your own brother-in-law, I believe, who champi-
oned women's capability in making good sense," she smiled
back. "No, I admire Angelina Weld and Sarah Grimke greatly.
Especially when you consider they could have had anything
they wanted from the system of the South. With Judge Grimke
of South Carolina for a father—why, every worldly comfort
was theirs to ask for. But they chose to go against all that and
become abolitionists. They were willing to sacrifice all for
their vision. I. . .I admire that," she finished quietly.

"But?"

"But what?"

"You feel something other than admiration, but you didn't
say it. Is there something you don't approve of?"

"No, I just, well, I do more than admire them. I envy them.
But we're not supposed to envy, are we? It's just that, they're
so certain. And they're doing such great and important things."

"And you're not?"

"I?" she laughed. "I hardly think keeping house and. . .and
keeping volcanic young misses in hand," she glanced back at
where Margaret was again the center of a merry group of young
people, "qualifies as great."

He thought a moment. "Who was it, do you know, that
inspired the Grimkes to become abolitionist speakers? Who
planted that seed to rebel against their upbringing and make that
sacrifice?"

"I don't know. I've never heard." .

"Who do you suppose, for instance, brought Charles Finney to
the Lord?"

She shook her head, "I'm afraid I don't know that either. We can be very grateful to whoever it was, though."

"Exactly. I don't know either. Who does know? They're probably some unknown people who just—just kept houses and gave advice to fiery young people." He smiled. "But we can have no idea what may come of that advice. Do you really think your smile of encouragement to little Johnnie Dougherty pleases the Lord less than Angelina Grimke Weld's best speech? Sure, there's a place for great public works. But some unknown person—lots of them I'll bet—is behind every one person who gets all the attention.

"Besides," he said, looking out over the river again, "there's a lot of work for the Kingdom that can't be trumpeted out loud. Some has to be done by people who go along quietly, not calling attention to themselves, but always being there."

Sarah opened her mouth to ask what he meant, but something kept the question inside. "The ladies look like they're packing up. I guess we'd best get back. I should go get my things. And my sister, wherever she is!" She lifted her skirts to step through the grasses and remaining wildflowers on the hillside and bent to pick a fading Queen Anne's lace.

"That's one of the nice things about living here. You can't wander through a meadow of wildflowers in the city. It's all houses and roads and new buildings on every square inch of space. There's something very freeing about wildflowers." She spun the stem around in her hand, and held it up. "They look so delicate—yet they just sprout up anywhere and weather the worst conditions—storms, frost, heat. And they just keep coming back for more, turning their faces to the sun and making people happy to see them."

"Kind of like you, Sarah," he said, and waved good-bye as he walked toward his departing family.

nine

"And how is the music teacher doing?" Sarah teased as she entered the small cabin Hannah called home. It was only one room—the church couldn't afford much. But Hannah had made it warm and comfortable, from the quilt-covered bed in one corner to the large desk by the fire where she did her school-work. The desk was bare of ornamentation save a large daguerrotype of a certain young man. It hadn't taken Sarah long to determine who that was and to give her opinion of William as a fine-looking man, sturdy enough for deepest, darkest Africa.

It was not at the desk that Hannah now sat. Instead, she occupied one of her two unmatched chairs, her hands busy with a beautiful creation of needlework roses and lace.

"For your trousseau? A bit fancy for Africa, don't you think?"

Hannah smiled as her fingers kept at the delicate work. "No. It's for the fair next week. Are you going?"

"Yes. I think I'm going with you actually. You're going with Pastor and Rachel?"

"Uh um." She nodded as she bit a stray string. "The whole Winston clan," she smiled.

"So are Margaret and I. Papa's too busy, so they took pity on us two girls. Are you going to exhibit that?"

"No, no. Not I. It's to sell. A group of ladies gathers fancy stitching, rugs, quilts, that sort of thing to sell at the fair for . . .for charity."

"A group here? Why haven't I heard of it? I'd love to help." Sarah cleared the other chair of its assorted books and sat down.

Hannah looked up at her and spoke slowly. "Word is, this

group of ladies wouldn't exactly be welcome in your home."

"What word? Whom could I possibly not welcome?" Sarah looked puzzled and hurt.

"Not you, Mr. Brown." Hannah put her sewing down. "Sarah, you're my best friend, and I trust you completely, but you must not repeat what I tell you about what I'm doing with this." She indicated the pillow in her lap.

Sarah blinked. "Of course," she stammered. "But how could sewing be so serious?"

"The 'group' of ladies is the Female Anti-Slavery Society of Alton. They sell things at the fair to raise money for. . .for items that slaves might need who are. . .passing through."

"Passing through, Hannah? You mean they raise money for the Underground Railroad?"

"Yes. The colored folk come through here with barely tatters on their backs, usually. Society women can sew clothes for them—and do. But they can't sew shoes. So the money from fairs goes for that and for other things."

"I see. I gather that if the particular ladies' names were common knowledge they might have trouble?"

"Some might. Some are very outspoken and willing to be known in the town as abolitionists, but others aren't. There's too much at stake for both them and those they help. To be known would be to endanger any 'guests' they might entertain from Missouri. They don't usually mention at the booth what they're selling things for. One doesn't exactly go around leaving public record of being an Underground Railroad supporter."

"No, I suppose not. I begin to see the danger here I've been warned of. Papa's opinions on the subject—well-known opinions I'm sure if I know Papa—surely would leave my feelings appearing uncertain. I can see why I wasn't told."

"You know now. Are you still willing? I know those fingers are as good as mine at sewing."

Sarah pursed her lips in thought. "I don't know. It wouldn't exactly be disobeying Papa if I didn't tell him. But that's probably disobedience in spirit, isn't it? I mean, to do what I know he would forbid if he knew. It just seems. . .still wrong, I guess."

Hannah resumed her sewing. "Your father isn't a believer?"

"No. Why?"

"Because the things of the dark hate the things of light. They always will. It's going to be very difficult for you to please God and him at the same time."

Sarah nodded. "I just don't know when one thing supersedes another. When is it really God's will that I disobey for a good reason? I wonder how Mama did it, being married to him. That must be the hardest life I can imagine, being married to a man who doesn't share your beliefs—why, your very reason for living! I'd always feel there was a barrier between us, and I'd always be worried for his soul. I know Mama was."

"I'm very glad I found a man more devoted to God than even to me. I know then if he's following God he'll always be committed to his pledge for my welfare. If I hadn't found someone like that, I'd still be waiting." Hannah smiled a dreamy smile at the picture on the desk. Sarah could tell she was miles away, thinking perhaps of the day her union with her fiancé would finally take place. She kept quiet so as not to intrude on her friend's reverie.

A needle jab brought Hannah back to her cabin room. "Ow! That's what I get for not paying attention to what my hands are doing. Anyway, I hope it's fine weather for the fair. They say it's quite the highlight of the year."

"I know. I'm so excited to see it. It will be very different from fairs back east, no doubt. I remember going to one in New York. It was very dazzling with the raree-shows and waxworks and all. But I'm kind of looking forward to something more in keeping with the peaceful fields of my new Illinois home. And David and Ellen won't tell me a thing about what to expect!"

"And you'll enjoy it even more, being surprised. I know you."

Sarah laughed, "Yes, you do." She stood up. "I'm afraid I can't stay. I stopped to drop off some of my old piano books. I thought they might help you teach notes and things. But I need to go over to the church now and practice for a while. I promised to play for services for a few weeks, while Mrs. Ryan's hip is healing. A bad fall she had. I took some stew and bread over there the day before yesterday, and she still looked quite tired. Hope she's up and better soon."

❧

Fair day dawned with an unpromising gray sky. Sarah frowned out her window. "I did so want my first fair day in my new home to be perfect." She moved to look for a dress appropriate for the drizzling weather. "Oh, well. It's only a little rain, after all. I'm sure it can't stop me from enjoying myself." Throwing the light green dress she chose over her head, she tied her long brown hair back with a matching ribbon. "No sense in putting it up. With all the bouncing around and walking and wind and rain—no hairpins ever made could withstand that." She looked longingly at the light slippers she had planned to wear. "No, not today. Not exactly practical for rain." Sighing, she picked up the sturdy walking shoes she had never cared much for and pattered down the stairs.

"It's raining!" wailed Margaret, coming in late for breakfast. "I wanted to wear my prettiest summer dress and stay outside all day! Instead, there's this old thing." She waved a disgusted hand at her yellow muslin dress. "You'd be pleased, Sarah. I'm being sensible for once and wearing this." She slumped into her place.

Sarah smiled at her sister's distress. She knew that as soon as Margaret reached the fairgrounds her mood would change dramatically. Margaret never stayed down for long. In fact, Sarah chuckled to herself, she never stayed in one frame of mind at all for very long.

"I know," she replied. "I wanted the same thing. But it will clear up, and you look lovely anyway."

"You think so?" Margaret brightened. "Maybe I'll meet someone interesting today. . .some mysterious stranger, outside the fortune-teller's tent. . . ."

Sarah rolled her eyes. Yes, Margaret was already forgetting her gloom.

The rain did clear up by the time they reached the fairgrounds, crowded happily in George Winston's wagon, the sun still refused to make an appearance. Already the area buzzed with noise and confusion. Barkers loudly hawked their wares, while frazzled mothers called to children running lost in the crowds. Colors danced everywhere—from the boldly hued sideshow tents and painted clowns to the scarlet and purple skirts of showgirls running to their performances. From somewhere on the left, calliope music hooted its invitation.

"I want to see the acrobats!" enthused Margaret. "Will they walk on the high wire? Do you suppose they have rides? We rode an elephant in New York!" She paused briefly to let the sensation sink in. "Let's go, Sarah, let's go!" She pulled her sister's arm and strained toward the crowds.

"You and Joanna go ahead," said Mr. Winston. "The two of you will probably want to keep a much faster pace than the rest of us."

Margaret transferred her hold from her sister to Joanna.

"When shall we meet you, Papa?" asked the younger girl.

"Let's say return here at six o'clock. That should give us all plenty of time." He had barely finished when the two girls ran off into the noise and swirl. "Now Charlotte, don't you and Rachel have to be at the mission society booth soon?"

"Yes, we'd better go now and take our turn behind the table. The rest of you have a good time. We'll meet you here." The two couples walked off, leaving Sarah, David, Ellen, and Hannah to decide what attraction to visit first.

"It's busy and dazzling, yet. . .yet still homey," said Sarah as they waded into the fray. "More. . .more humble and human than big-city fairs." To her left, young men tried to flatten moving targets with small balls, while others tossed rings around pins with more or less success. She watched as one lucky fellow collected a large wooden bear on wheels for his efforts. "How will he ever carry it around all day?" she laughed. On the other side, showmen handled real bears and other animals in a small menagerie. The four stopped to watch the antics of a trained raccoon playing bells and a bear (caged, Sarah breathed thankfully) on a strange one-wheeled cycle.

They passed politicians on wooden boxes, promising a better government; improbable doctors promising better health; and zealots promising the end of the world.

"Ladies," crooned a voice close to Sarah's left. "Your fortune told for only a dime. Just ten cents will tell you what you wish to know about life—love, family, fortune." A small woman with gossamer purple and green material covering her head and body, bedecked all over with gold chains, directed them toward a dark tent. "Come," she beckoned at Sarah. "You wish to know your future, don't you?"

Sarah paused, blinking at the wildness of the woman before her. For one moment, she wished she could believe in the woman's ability, and the carefree world she epitomized. The future—her place in it. Oh, that it could be given her in a simple few minutes for only a dime. "No." She smiled at the woman. "That is, yes, I'd love to know, but no, God knows, and I guess He'll tell me when it's best." She smiled again, not wanting to offend the woman, but glad in her refusal.

When they tired of the barrage of sight and sound, the four took refuge in the relatively quiet display of ribbon-winning cookery and handwork. "Isn't that lovely?" Sarah's attention was caught by a particularly arresting quilt proudly bearing a grand-prize ribbon. A simple double wedding ring pattern, its perfectly matched rainbow of blue and rose hues showed an artist's touch. "The stitching is just exquisite!" She bent closer to inspect.

"And she is a good judge," added Hannah. "I've seen enough of her work to be impressed."

"Why. . ." Sarah stood open-mouthed, looking at the quilt's tag. "Why, this is your own mother's work!" She looked accusingly at David. "Why didn't you say so?"

"Because it's much nicer to hear you praise it without knowing whose it is." He chuckled. "Mother could have flown home last week when they pronounced it a grand-prize winner. She didn't come out of the air for days."

"You ought to enter one next year, Sarah," Hannah told her. "You'd win a ribbon for sure."

"I don't know. It's so. . .scary to think of putting one's own handwork on display—to be judged by everyone who goes by. If I didn't win a prize, I'd be discouraged, and if I did, I'd be wondering how many people looked at it and thought I shouldn't have."

Ellen nodded. "Me too. I'd be much too frightened."

"You ought not be," her brother said. "You've inherited Mother's talent. But I think, if you ladies are finished here, it's time to find something to eat. Always an adventure here." He winked at Sarah. "So many kinds of food—some we're not quite sure what they are." He led the way back into the noise, and the host of tantalizing smells Sarah could now detect from all directions. She lagged a step behind the others, savoring the air.

A flash of orange and white caught her attention as it disappeared behind a barrel off to her right. Moving away from the others, Sarah went to investigate. A small, wild-eyed kitten peeked back at her as she leaned over the barrel. Dirty orange stripes covered its body, leaving room only for four white paws and a white-tipped nose. Its dusty fur clung to tiny bones—a silent testimony to the animal's hunger.

"Oh! Poor little thing," she cried. "Come here. Come to Sarah. You need someone to take care of you." She knelt carefully to scoop up the scrawny ball of fluff. Unused to kindness, the terrified animal mustered all of his strength to leap over her arm and back into the crowds.

"No! Come back! I won't hurt you!" She chased him a few yards, around wooden stalls and through a group of laughing children at a puppet theater. But it was a hopeless effort to find such a tiny thing among so many feet and skirts. "Oh, poor little lost baby," she mourned, leaning against a wooden game counter.

"Well, how do, pretty lady. How come you to be alone?" A stocky man about ten years her senior stood at her elbow. Though it was only afternoon, Sarah could tell by his close breath that he had drunk more than lemonade that day.

"I. . .I'm not alone," she stammered, looking about. She realized then with a slight pang of fear that in chasing the lost kitten she herself had gotten lost. She couldn't see her three friends anywhere.

"Wal, you look alone. C'mon. So'm I. Maybe I could buy you somethin' to eat or throw a ball and win ye one o' them nice prizes."

Sarah doubted that, in his present condition, he could hit the entire tent with a ball, let alone a small target.

He pulled at her arm. "C'mon little lady. We could have lots of fun here."

"Don't touch me!" she exclaimed and instinctively stamped on his foot. Letting go with a howl, he nearly fell backward. At the same time, she felt an arm go about her waist and heard a voice at her side.

"I believe, Sarah," said David, looking at the angry man, "we somehow lost you. But I'm sure you'd like to rejoin our party now, am I right?"

"Quite right," she leaned gratefully into his arm. David steered her away from the man, who suddenly decided he didn't want to risk his other foot by chasing after her anyway.

"Thank you," she breathed when they had gotten a few steps away. "I couldn't see any of you. I didn't know what to do."

"Looks to me like you did. That poor man won't be able to walk straight for days. What did you need me for?"

She smiled up at him, his humor restoring hers. "Why, because it would have ruined my ladylike reputation to have had to knock him in the dirt myself. What would people think?"

"I know what I think. I think I'd better remember for the future not to make you angry!"

She laughed and looked down at the detested solid walking shoes she hadn't wanted to wear. *Lord, You have a sense of humor,* she thought. *Light slippers would not have done for that at all!*

Just before leaving, David made the three girls stop at a last game booth. His sister already had two baby dolls he had won, one under each arm—one for her and one for the absent Joanna. Hannah too had her own prize, which she had won herself at the ring toss.

"This one is special," he said, picking up the three balls to be thrown through a small hole in the booth's backdrop. The first two missed, but the third sailed right through without touching the sides. "I want that one," he told the barker, pointing at a wooden kitten, painted orange and white. Sarah smiled. She had told them all her reason for getting lost and how sorry she had felt for the tiny, starved animal. "Sorry you couldn't have the real one," he said, handing the prize to her. "Hope this will do."

"At least I won't have to feed this one," she laughed shakily, trying not to cry. "Oh, but I hope someone does feed the other one."

ten

Sarah sat in her favorite place—the big bluff overlooking the river's endless expanse. She felt entitled to a holiday, so she had taken her dinner to the hill, wanting to relax and be alone for one afternoon.

The past few weeks had been hard work, but the area harvest was finished. Sarah enjoyed watching the men in the fields outside of town, so she had happily volunteered to help with meals for the teams of men nearby. She got a strange satisfaction from watching for the first time the green and gold piles the farmers made—tributes to God's generosity and care. She had to admit, however, she didn't like the dead stubble behind her now—the dreary emptiness of fields in fall.

Her own modest "harvest" of wildflowers hung in the drying room old Mrs. Crandall had loved. The cellar was full of the food she had traded for and bought in the past few weeks, stored carefully for the winter months. They had come too late to plant a garden, but next year she would have one. If, she realized, someone showed her how to plant and tend one. In these few short months in Illinois she had forgotten that this city-bred girl had never planted a garden—never put her hands in the dirt in her life! But she wanted to have her own harvest time and feeling of satisfaction in a cellar full of produce from her own hand. "And Yours," Sarah amended, looking up to the lazy clouds. "I know there's no producing anything without Your hand, Lord."

She turned back toward the river, her thoughts forming around the nagging question that had bothered her the last few weeks. "So what am I producing, Lord? Hannah's teaching and

65

going off to the mission field. Rachel and Anne are helping their husbands build churches. Somehow shelves full of food and flowers don't seem enough to show." She flopped down on her stomach, on her blanket near the grass, and studied an old yellowed stalk between her fingers. "Sometimes. . . sometimes I just feel as empty as those fields."

She rolled over on her back and gazed again at the sky. "You would know just what to say, wouldn't you, Mama? I have so many questions I wish you were here to answer. Did you wonder about your future when you were twenty? Did you wish for some important task? . . . No, I suppose not," she said after a moment's thought. "You were married and had Anne by the time you were twenty. You had your future—raising three girls who needed you. A task doesn't get much more important than that."

She looked down the hill and noticed in the distance a young woman playing with two small boys outside a neat little house. "Is that what I should do, Mama? Get married? It would certainly solve the problem of living with Papa." She smiled, re-membering Hannah's words to Harriet on that subject. "Rather drastic solution to a disagreeable father," she had said. Sarah agreed. But still—the idea of being cared for and being away from the tension of caring for others was very tempting. *Tempt-ing,* she told herself, *like the comfort of full barns in the fall— secure from the storms.* "I suspect that's what I like about harvest time, Mama," she admitted. "Everything is so terribly. . .unas-sailable.

"Anyway," she laughed, rolling back to her feet, "since no one has asked me or seems likely to, I guess I'm not in much danger of succumbing to that particular temptation." The image of David's protective arm around her at the fair flashed in her mind. She shook her head. No, there wasn't anything but friend-liness there, and that was just what she wanted.

"Even though, Liza O'Reilly, you seem to think otherwise,"

she said, putting her hands on her hips. Sarah still remembered the store owner's first accusation about girls coming west to "git 'em husbands." Mrs. O'Reilly had made several similar comments since. David was right—the lady did possess an amazingly busy tongue. *But perhaps she just needs someone to talk,* Sarah thought, lying back down on the soft blanket covering browning grass.

"Well, just for today I'm not going to worry about any of it. I'm going to enjoy what we have left of this beautiful Indian summer. Really, this is one season that's more-lovely here than back home, in spite of the stubble fields." She closed her eyes to the warm sun and smiled at the feel of a cool prairie breeze floating across her face.

"Seems as if I'm making a habit of coming across you sleeping."

Sarah sat up suddenly, shielding her eyes from the sun. "And startling me too," she retorted at David, who was standing over her. Her words came out a little sharper than she had intended.

"It was a shame to wake you, such a lovely picture you made all curled up in the sun with a smile on your face. What were you dreaming of to produce such a look?" he asked, sitting down next to her.

"I. . .I don't remember anything." She looked away and began to collect her things. "What are you doing here?"

"Your father told me I'd find you here. Or at least," he smiled, "he told me, 'She said something about taking some ridiculous picnic to an old hill.'" He gave a fair imitation of Papa's voice and no-nonsense manner. "I gathered from that you were here, seeing as this is your favorite 'old hill.' I came with an invitation from Mother for you to come to supper with us and then spend the evening practicing with Ellen, since you two are to sing tomorrow in church."

"Oh!" Sarah put her hand to her mouth. "I had completely

forgotten. I suppose I must come. . .I mean," she paused, realizing that sounded rather ungracious. "I mean I'd love to and I must," she smiled. "But. . .I'm afraid I haven't even made supper for Papa and Margaret yet. I've just had a lazy day, and now I'll pay for it."

"Can't Margaret do that? She's what, sixteen now? I assume by sixteen she knows how to get the family's supper now and then."

"I suppose she might know but. . .well, knowing and doing are different things."

"If you don't give her a choice, she'll have to do it. Let her try—you have to sometime."

"But what if. . . ."

He held up his hand to stop her. "Don't worry about the 'what if's.' What if she fails? Then she learns something. Come on."

"But I could help her. . . ."

"Sarah," he paused. "Sarah, you worry so much about Margaret not growing up to be responsible. But do you think perhaps. . . well, maybe sometimes you hover over her so much she never gets a chance to try?"

"I. . .what do you mean?" she asked, feeling a little hurt by his words.

He plucked a dying flower from the grass and began to pull its faded petals. "I know you've had to raise her through the toughest years. I know you feel responsible for her—like a mother yourself. But holding too tightly might just produce the rebellion you're afraid of. I'm sure, after all, that the values you and your mother instilled aren't likely to go far wrong."

Sarah remained silent, thinking. She gave a short, amused sigh and shook her head. "Holding her too tightly isn't even really possible anymore. She's past letting me. But maybe you're right. Maybe it's my trying so hard that she hates. Perhaps she's old enough now that I need to switch to friend rather than older sister."

"It's worth a try." He shrugged. "I don't pretend to be an expert but. . . ."

"Then I guess tonight's as good a time as any to begin. I'll let her be more responsible—or insist on it, since 'allowing' Margaret to get supper means it wouldn't be done unless she does indeed have no choice! However," she added, standing to go, "I may be hearing from Papa about it when he gets cold beans and bread for supper!"

"I'm glad you agree, because I already told them, when I was there, that you wouldn't be back," he said, gathering her blanket and basket over one arm.

"And what if I said I resented having my decisions made for me?" she asked in mock indignation.

"I'd say that's the independent spirit I knew you had in you. Maybe you'll be an Angelina Grimke yet." He grinned.

"It's a good thing Papa lost his fortune then anyway," she said, "because if I did that I'd surely be disowned."

They climbed into the waiting buggy, and David flipped the reins to signal the horses. He was silent for a moment, then asked, "So that's why you moved here?"

She looked confused. "What?"

"You never mentioned anything about losing a fortune before."

"Oh. I. . .I didn't mean to mention it now. I shouldn't have."

"Then I guess I shouldn't have asked."

"No, I don't mind. It's just. . .Papa doesn't want it known. He tries to look prosperous. He's doing fine now but. . .not as he would like to be doing. Not as he once was. And it's very hard for him to accept. Yes, that's why we moved here. Everything he owned back east is gone. And what he had here is all that was left."

"So that's why he's so insistent that you be a 'proper young lady.' Because that's the life you were raised for."

"Yes, I suppose I was," she reflected. "But that life meant different things to Papa and Mama. She still wanted us to find something useful to do with our lives. But Papa didn't believe in educating women 'beyond their sphere' or filling their minds with too many opinions. What he would have said if he had found out Mama and I read his papers after him!"

He laughed, "I can imagine. My mother and sisters not only read them—they debate them with me. And win!"

She smiled and shook her head. "Well, we had no one with whom to debate. So I never knew if the opinions I formed could hold up."

He pulled the team to a stop in front of the house. "Actually," he said, going around to help her down, "I think you'll find things different here. On the frontier men need the women to work beside them. When you're trying to scrape a living from the wilderness, any hand is a welcome one. And any opinions are worth listening to."

"Well, someone should tell Papa that!" She laughed. "'A lady's place is home and hearth, and the less knowledge she puts into her head, the less discontent she'll be there.'" She parroted the words she and her sisters had all heard when they had begged to be allowed to finish more schooling.

"Then you've no wish for a home and hearth?" he asked.

"I didn't mean. . .I just. . . ." She looked down at her hands, flustered at the suddenly personal question. Ellen appeared at the door, and Sarah waved hello. "I think I'll find your mother and see if I can be of any help. At least this proper lady did learn to cook." She laughed slightly, walking briskly to the kitchen of the Winston home.

❧

"I'm very glad you had the foresight to choose a song, Ellen." After a wonderful supper they had practiced their piece for the morrow several times over. Then Sarah had remained chatting with the family until well into the evening. She didn't know how the time had passed so quickly, but it was late indeed as they sat around the table, drinking coffee and talking. "I'm so sorry I forgot about our duet. It's been quite a week!"

"Obviously you don't need much time to learn music. It must come very naturally to you." Mrs. Winston smiled, handing her another cup of coffee.

Sarah blushed. "I've always loved to sing. I guess just doing it for so long makes me able to learn new things quickly. Of course, this piece isn't exactly new to me."

A light rap came on the door, so faint Sarah wasn't sure she'd heard it. *It's certainly late for visitors,* she thought. *I hope it isn't Papa come to find* me! She flushed at the embarrassing thought.

"Who's there?" called Mr. Winston, starting for the door.

"Friend of a frien'," came the tentative voice from outside the hallway entrance.

Mr. Winston stopped, his outstretched arm faltering at the parlor doorway. His wife put a hand to her mouth. Even young Joanna looked at Sarah oddly. In fact, Sarah suddenly found herself the center of a circle of frightened, uncertain eyes.

"Don't worry about Sarah, Father," said David finally. "Besides, you haven't much choice."

Bewildered, she watched as Charles Winston nodded and went out to open the door. Through the parlor entrance they could see a young colored woman nearly collapse into the hallway, a sleeping child in her arms.

"Come in. You're among friends."

With what seemed the last of her energy, the woman stepped into the room, shying from the bright lamplight. Mrs. Winston reached for the child to relieve her of one burden. Instinctively, she pulled back, wrapping her arms tighter around the small bundle. "No!" came her exhausted cry.

"It's all right." Mrs. Winston touched her thin shoulder soothingly and steered her toward the fire. "I'll not harm her. She'll stay right here with you. But you need rest."

The terrified woman scanned the room, as if, from any

corner, someone might leap out to steal her precious load. Finally, reassured by the compassionate faces she saw, she relinquished the little girl and slumped in a heap on the carpet beside the fire. She remained there, staring into the flames as if in a trance.

Ellen disappeared quietly and returned several minutes later with the warmed remains of their supper. She knelt by the woman—*not much more than a girl really*, thought Sarah, *but still a mother.*

"Here," Ellen whispered. "You'll feel better with some hot food inside of you." The girl transferred her unseeing gaze to the plate and then to the face above it.

"Thank ya," she said softly. "Thank y' all," she added, looking around. "I. . .I's sorry, I jest. . .don't mind when I. . .we . . .was last warm." She pulled her meager clothing closer and looked back at the plate, as if she half expected it to disappear.

"What's your name?" asked Joanna, coming to drape a blanket around the woman's shoulders.

"Esther. An' that," she pointed at her child still sleeping in Mrs. Winston's arms, "be Lizbeth." Sarah shuddered at the look on her face as she spoke of her daughter. What could have caused that expression—a mixture, it seemed, of both anguish and love?

It took very few minutes for her to finish the food before her. They could only wonder about the last time that thin body had had a good meal. "Thank ya," she said again, as Ellen cleared the dishes away.

"Tell us why you've run away, Esther," Mrs. Winston prodded after the girl seemed to revive. "Tell us about you and Elizabeth."

"Maybe you'd better take Sarah home, David," his father said, still uneasy.

"No, please." She held up her hand. "I want to hear. You've nothing to fear from me. Please let me stay."

"Perhaps she should, Father," David spoke up. A look of understanding passed between the two men, and the elder nodded.

"Yes, then, do stay."

"We come from down M'ssourah," Esther began. "Purty far ways down, I be guessin'. Been runnin' nine days. I left so fast. Weren't no time for food or clothes. Didn't have none to spare anyway."

"Did you come alone?" Mrs. Winston asked.

"Yes'm. Jest me an Lizbeth."

"But—how dangerous!"

"I done had to go, ma'am. Had to get outta that place fast. My baby. . . ," and her voice broke.

"It's all right. You're safe now. Go on."

"But I'm not safe!" she cried. "We won't be safe til we get to Canada! An' we has to get there fast, 'cause dey're lookin' for us!"

Unable to deny the truth of this statement, Mrs. Winston remained silent. Enough runaway slaves had been returned to misery after reaching free Illinois because of men who pretended to be their friends. Canada was, indeed, her only true safety. There she and her child would remain free without fear.

"You must have had good reason to take such a risk. Were you afraid for Elizabeth?"

The woman nodded. "She be all I got, ma'am. Maybe he figures 'cause he could make me have her he could take her 'way. But he can't! She be my own chile! No one can take 'way my Lizzie!"

Ellen patted her hand in reassurance. "Of course not. Not here. But what happened?"

"I. . .I be a housemaid for the mas'r an missus. Served 'em good with no trouble. But mas'r—he studied as I be too likely lookin' to be jest a maid. I said I jest wanted to be a decent girl! I try to stay 'way from him. But I never got a choice. He'd a killed me in the field if I didn' do what he say—he done told me so. I couldn't. . . ." She hid her face in her hands. "Then I had Lizbeth," she continued, "an' he stayed 'way from me after dat. The missus, she got jealous. He try to tell her it be another slave's baby chile. But she knowed. An' she hated me for it. She beat me ev'ry time she got de chance, an' give me heaps o' work I couldn't do, and beat me if it weren't done. She wouldn't never let me go to mah babe when she's cryin'. Den I. . .I heared her tellin' mas'r she made a deal wi' a trader comin' through. She done sold mah baby down to New O'leans! I knows what dey do to girls dere. Dey takes 'em half white, like my baby, cuz dat make de men like 'em more. It don't matter how young she be. Dey'll raise her to it. I'd die afore I let 'em do dat to my chile! She be better dead too. . . ."

"So you ran before they could come for her."

Her chin came up, proud despite her tears. "Yes'm. I run 'way. An dey'll never catch me an her 'live."

"Not if we can help it, Esther." Ellen squeezed her hand. "I'll go see to a place for you to sleep."

"I don't know what the talk around town is about runaways right now," Mr. Winston broke in. "I'll see what I can hear tomorrow—see what kind of danger you might be in. That'll tell how long you should stay here. But tonight you hold your little Elizabeth and sleep safely. The Lord will let no harm come to you under my roof."

"The Lor' bless ya then, sir," she whispered.

The image of the woman's proudly desperate face haunted Sarah on the way home. Neither she nor David had spoken since they left the house, where Esther now slept in temporary peace. Sarah was afraid to speak because of the choking feeling threatening any sound she tried to make. She was afraid, too, of her jumbled emotions and what they might mean. Lowering her head, she let the tears begin silently. David noticed and stopped the horses.

"Go ahead and cry, Sarah. I'm sure I did the first time I heard such a story." His understanding words broke her last restraint. Accepting the solace of a comforting arm, she wept against him until the storm of her chaotic feelings subsided.

He handed her a handkerchief. "Do you want to talk about

it now?"

She sniffed and opened her eyes. "Oh, David, I've always known it was horrible. I've always felt for those people on the runaway flyers. But I. . .I've never met one. I've never seen the pain in one's face. The poor woman. . . ." She closed her eyes tightly to stop new tears.

"Hers is only one of many stories. All horrible. We've heard enough to know."

She looked up. "I thought it seemed everyone had performed those roles before. Then your house—your family—is part of the Underground Railroad?" He nodded, looking for her reaction. "But I don't understand. You told me. . .you said you had no opinion about abolitionists. 'Anybody can have whatever belief he wants, so long as I don't have to be involved,' you said. And you're involved up to your. . .your. . . ."

"My neck in it? Yes, and probably over my head. I told you before this isn't a safe town to air antislavery sentiment in openly. Even to you."

"But I told you how I felt."

"Yes. But you're from a slave district. Your father's opinions are well-known. There are those who would give a great deal to find out who hosts stations on the Underground Railroad in this area. It wouldn't be the first time a pretty girl was used to get that kind of information."

"And you thought that of me?"

"I didn't want to. I didn't believe it, really. You have many abilities, Sarah, but lying isn't among them. But. . .what if I were wrong? It's not just my own well-being I'd be risking. My whole family—and all those they help—would be jeopardized."

She looked out in thought at the cold night sky. "I understand. But now you've decided I'm to be trusted?"

He laughed slightly. "We didn't have much choice, did we? Should we have turned her away at the door and told you she was a midnight peddler?" He shook his head. "You may not be able to lie well enough to be a spy, but you're not exactly senseless. However. . . ," he sobered again, "my father will want more assurance than my belief in your character. He will want your word no one will ever know of this."

"Of course! Why, I could never. . . ." She looked shocked. "Why, you're my Christian brothers and sisters at least! And that poor woman. . . ."

"I know. But he would want me to ask."

"Yes." She nodded again. "I guess I can understand that." She paused. "But I'm frightened. It's all so. . .so. . .unreal. Of course one hears all about the Underground Railroad back east. I could hardly live in Washington and not know of it. But then it was some. . .some romantic story. Face to face with people I know, it's. . .scary. And illegal. And I'm not sure I can. . .can accept that. Is it ever all right to break the law, even if it's for a good reason?"

"A valid question." He frowned. "The law of the land is important—very important. But sometimes a man—or a woman," he looked down at her, "has to follow a higher law. Sometimes his conscience won't let him be at peace unless he steps out to heed what's more important. I'm not saying everyone must agree with what we're doing. But I'm convinced God would not have us turn our backs on those who flee to us for protection."

"How can you be so sure of that?"

"For one thing, the Bible says, 'Thou shalt not deliver unto his master the servant which is escaped from his master unto thee.' Deuteronomy twenty three, verse fifteen."

"But it also says to obey our government—and our parents. Those are commands I've tried to follow all my life. Tried hard too—considering Papa! I don't need to tell you what he'd say to my becoming an abolitionist! So which commands do I obey?"

"I can't answer that for you. I can only tell you my decision. You'll have to ask God for yours. Obey the one you can't not obey." He paused. "And if you were to decide to help with the cause, Sarah, there's plenty of need for someone like you. If you're still looking for an important work for the Lord."

She shook her head. "I don't know. It's all so confusing." She buried her head in her hands. "Oh, it's not at all the romantic picture it seems from the outside, is it?"

"No, not at all. It's the terrifying fact of those three men rotting in a Southern jail. But if it's the right thing to do in God's eyes, we must do it and leave the consequences to Him. You just do it."

"But if it's not right? To take such risks. . . ." The vision of the wives and children of those three men, all alone, flashed before her. What sort of grieved panic must they be experiencing? Their husbands and fathers might never return. "No!" she cried suddenly. "That can't be right! Surely God would rather we helped the slaves legally. I can't go against Papa like that. Or the law. I just can't!"

He made no answer. She turned back to him. "Have you. . . have you ever gone over to Missouri, as they did. . .to tell slaves of freedom?"

"Yes. I have." She gasped. "Not often. But yes. I'm one of the men your father would like to see hanged."

She met his eyes then and saw the silent withdrawal he made from her. His words revealed the sudden barrier between them, almost as if it were visible. At the same time she saw another emotion in his face—one she had never seen there before, but that spoke clearly of what might have been. Biting her lip, Sarah turned away and stumbled out of the buggy, not waiting for a hand down. She only knew she had to leave quickly, to forget what she had seen just now.

"I. . .I'm sorry. I have to go now. It's late and. . . ." She was already halfway to the door, running from the devils trying to change her mind. "Good night." She opened the door, rushing into the familiar light of home and safety.

He sat in the dark for a long moment. "Good-bye, Sarah," he said finally, and turned the team slowly away.

eleven

Sarah woke the next morning, hoping she had dreamed the events of last night. But no, her aching head and dry eyes reminded her quickly of the long hours spent in tossing confusion. When she had finally fallen asleep, her dreams had been worse still. She remembered snatches of them here and there. Faceless people in a huge, dark pit, calling out to her for help, pulling on her—she resisting the blackness, the fall. She remembered screaming, "Let me go!" and waking up, unable to sleep again for a long time. But last night hadn't been a dream.

"Ohhhh. . . ." Sarah moaned, sitting up on her bed. She massaged her back awkwardly with one hand, closing her eyes. "I don't think I'll ever be able to straighten up again." Groaning, she stood and walked to the small looking glass near her wardrobe. Red, sleepless eyes stared back.

"Do I really have to get up?" she asked her reflection. Her eyes lit upon the Bible and small hymnal beside her on the desk. She clapped one hand over her mouth. "Yes! I do! I have to sing this morning! Oh—why not any day but this?"

Sarah turned quickly to the wardrobe, riffling through dresses. "Not that one. It's too cool. And that one has a tear." She paused at her favorite blue wool. "No. I'm sick of that one." Her inventory ended with rejection of all candidates, for one reason or another. Turning away impatiently, Sarah plopped down before her glass. "At least I can do my hair," she grumbled. But that too proved unsatisfactory, as she combed and brushed and pinned furiously several times, only to yank the pins out again and fling them on the table.

She sighed heavily. "Obviously, the problem is me, not my hair."

Again she glanced at the small black Bible. "Maybe if I have my devotions first I'll be in a better mood to go to church." She opened the worn pages carefully to Jeremiah—the book she had been study-ing the past few months. She had decided that, as an "exile" to a foreign land herself, perhaps she could learn something from this great prophet. Today though, she approached even her Bible with-out enthusiasm. What could Jeremiah have to say about the ques-tions that haunted her this morning?

"Forgive me, Lord. I know I'm distracted and disgruntled. It's not fair to come to You in a bad mood and expect You to magically make it disappear. Help me to learn something from You in spite of myself."

" 'Thus saith the Lord. . .unto all that are carried away unto Babylon. . . .' " Sarah began reading.

"That's me," she grumbled.

" 'Build ye houses, and dwell in them; and plant gardens, and eat the fruit of them. . . .' "

"Why, so I've done," she answered. "The house is nice and settled now, and I'm waiting to plant a garden just as soon as I can."

" '. . .and give your daughters to husbands, that they may bear sons and daughters. . .' "

"Well, perhaps I won't do that part just. . .just yet."

" 'Seek the peace of the city whither I have caused you to be, . . .and pray for it.' "

"Seek peace—what does that mean if not obey the laws? Well, here it is, just as plain as I could want. Obedience to government must come first. You just have to obey the rules and trust God to make everything else work out." The faceless images of her dream floated before her, along with Esther's tortured eyes. She snapped the Bible shut. "That's what it says! I've got to believe it! I asked God to show me the truth, and He did."

Whirling away, she snatched the first dress she found and began changing her clothes. It was an old purple poplin whose color didn't suit her and that she had never really liked. She shrugged one shoulder in defiance and put it on anyway. Pulling her hair back into a tight knot, she jabbed the pins into the coil, grabbed her books, and ran down the stairs, her aching bones protesting at every determined footfall.

She met her father coming in the front door from the stable. "Breakfast ready yet?"

"No, Papa. I'm sorry. I overslept. But I'll have it done very soon." Sarah clanged pans hurriedly onto the stove. The cornmeal she began measuring into one spilled from the bag in a rush all over. Growling impatiently, she wiped the mess to one side, then went in search of some eggs and the slab of ham her father preferred in the morning. "Ouch!" she yelled, banging her head on the way into the food cellar. Emerging with the eggs, she set them to boiling and threw the ham in a pan to sizzle. "No time to make biscuits," she said. "I'll just have to use the rest of the bread I made Friday. It will be dry but. . . ." She searched for the remains of the loaf she knew she had left yesterday. "It's gone! Wouldn't you just expect that? I wonder if they did have cold beans and bread last night?"

One boiled-over pot of coffee and burnt pan of cornmeal later, Sarah placed breakfast on the table. This morning she was past caring what it tasted like. The two of them had nearly finished when Margaret bounced in, late as usual.

"You don't look so good this morning, Sarah. And where did you get that ugly dress?"

Sarah's hands curled tightly as she struggled to keep back tears. "Excuse me, I've got to hurry. I have to sing this morning and can't be late." She snatched her things and dashed out the door, leaving the breakfast mess on the table.

"God," she began, when safely out the door, "the way I see it I have two choices. I can go back to bed and have a good cry, or I can take myself in hand and be reasonable." She paused, mustering the energy to do the latter. "I know Margaret didn't intend to be mean—it's just her way. And," she admitted, looking down with a wry laugh, "the dress *is* ugly."

Sarah succeeded in producing a smile before she reached the church door. She also succeeded in avoiding David—a task, she realized with a sigh, made easier by the fact that he showed no inclination to speak to her. She hated to be grateful for someone else's misfortune, but she was glad to be at the piano due to Mrs. Ryan's hip injury and not in the Winston pew. Only once, near the church steps after services, did they find themselves close to one another.

"Miss Brown, Miss Brown!" an eager Johnnie Dougherty tugged at her sleeve as she exited the building. "Do you know the story about the fiery furnace?"

Sarah bent down to his eye level. "I do. But I'm not sure if I remember it all. Can you tell it to me?"

"It's a great story! All about these three fellows—Shadrach, Meshach, and Ab. . .Adeb. . .Abedingo!" Sarah smiled. It was a pretty fair try for a six-year-old.

"And what did these three fellows do?" she asked.

"Well the king—he was a bad king." Johnnie scowled to demonstrate. "He made this big stat. . .statchoo. And he made it the law that everyone had to bow to the. . .the. . .to it. But these three fellows knew God wouldn't want them to do that—so they said no!" He shouted the last word and paused to wait for her appreciation.

"So what happened to them?"

"That's the good part! The king got real mad." He scowled again, looking as fierce as a freckle-faced six-year-old could. "And he threw them in a big fiery furnace—I guess that's kind of like a big cookin' stove, huh?"

Sarah nodded. "A very big one."

"And they were s'posed to die 'cause they disobeyed the law."

"That sounds very bad for them," she said seriously.

"Yah! But they didn't! God saved 'em 'cause they did what was right and listened to Him instead of the king! Ain't that a great story?"

Sarah felt David's eyes on her, and she looked up.

"Yes, a great story, Johnnie, great indeed," she said, noticing David turning away. Sarah nodded and turned away as well to start her walk home—a walk that suddenly felt empty and lonely as the brown grass around her.

twelve

"Glad you're home early, Sarah," Papa said as she walked in their parlor. "Forgot to tell you—I'm expecting a guest for dinner."

Sarah hid her frown. She was in no humor for company. "A guest, Papa? Who?"

"A Mr. Morris. Glenn Morris. Owns some land just across the river. I ship some of his goods up north. A fine man. Thought we ought to get better acquainted."

Sarah looked at her father suspiciously. She had read his tone and face long enough to know there was something he wasn't telling her about this guest. She shrugged and turned toward the stairs. *I also know he won't tell me, either, no matter how I ask,* she thought. She wasn't really very interested in a dinner full of business talk anyway.

When Glenn Morris came to the door, however, she decided to reconsider. A young man with blue eyes and curling blond hair, he soon made it clear he had come to socialize, not work.

"So these are Miss Sarah and Miss Margaret," he said to Papa, stepping in the entryway. "Beautiful ladies indeed, just as you said. But I can hardly tell which is the elder."

Sarah blushed and Margaret beamed. It was a remark calculated to please both of them. "Welcome, Mr. Morris." Sarah extended her hand. "Won't you come sit down? Dinner will be ready very soon."

Their guest appeared happy to answer questions about himself throughout dinner. Margaret, never one to shy away when she wanted to know something, kept up much of the exchange. "How can you be a landowner and be so young?" she asked.

"You can't be over thirty!" Sarah had wondered the same thing, but would never have asked.

"I am, in fact, exactly thirty." He smiled. "And my fortune of being wealthy is due to the misfortune of my father's death last year."

"I'm so sorry," Sarah automatically reacted. "We've lost a parent too, so we understand what you must feel."

"Yes, so your father told me. Told me you run the entire household, top to bottom now," Glenn turned to Sarah. "And do a bang-up job of it too. Judging by this pumpkin pie," he said, helping himself to a second piece, "I've no doubt it's true." Sarah looked at her father in wonder. Had he really said that? She hadn't thought he even noticed her work. He had certainly never told her she did a "bang-up job."

"Yes," he continued, "I'll miss Father. My mother died long ago—I was only nine. I hardly remember her. Father never remarried. He had a maid and a cook and he brought someone in to teach my older sisters. Guess he never felt the need for another wife. But my sisters are married, and it's all fallen to me now."

"And the business has all fallen to me. That's what I call a fair arrangement," crowed her Papa. "Shall we move to the parlor for more comfortable conversation? No, Sarah," he motioned to her as she began to collect the dishes. "Leave them. You come along—we need you too." For the second time that evening she stared at him. Why was Papa behaving so strangely tonight?

But the biggest surprise came later that evening after their guest had left. She sat quietly stitching at a project she needed to complete soon. Hannah's birthday was next week, and Sarah planned to surprise her with a pair of pretty scarves to throw over her two unmatched second-hand chairs. *At least,* she thought, *that would make them look more like a set.*

"What did you think of our guest, Sarah?" asked Papa, sitting down across from her.

"He seemed very nice," she replied noncommittally, paying

more attention to her sewing than the conversation. She stuck the needle in her mouth to work at a stubborn knot.

"I'm glad you think so, because we'll be seeing a lot of him. He asked for my permission to call on you, and I agreed. He'll be back this Wednesday night."

Sarah dropped the needle with a gasp. "He what?! Ouch!!" The lost needle jabbed her hand as she started in surprise. "But I don't even know the man!" She sucked at her wounded palm. "Why didn't he ask me?"

"Because," his voice rose slightly, "he's a gentleman who knows a girl's father is the one to consult on such things. Would you have denied him?"

She thought for a moment. "No, I suppose not. He was very nice." She smiled, remembering the flow of compliments on her cooking skills. It had felt rather heady to be appreciated. "I guess I just wasn't ready for the idea." Some feeling she couldn't label rebelled at the thought of Mr. Morris calling on her—of anyone calling on her.

"Wednesday will be fine," she said, picking up her needlework and heading for her room. *I wonder what he would especially like this time,* she asked herself on the way up the stairs. *As long as my cooking is going to be praised I might as well live up to it. How about a nice plum cake?*

Mr. Morris—or Glenn, as she soon came to call him—did call that Wednesday. He also called that Saturday and every week after that. She enjoyed their conversations and occasional walks through town and the countryside, whenever it was warm enough to walk in the evening. The sun was setting earlier and earlier now, so evening walks became fewer. Sarah soon realized that she had become a focus of town gossip because of the young stranger from Missouri. "Droppin' one rich young man to snare another," she overheard Liza O'Reilly whisper one day to another woman at the counter. She wanted desperately to say she hadn't dropped anyone—that she and David had never been more than family friends. But obviously the verdict on her had already been passed. Explaining away gossip would only feed the fire more, she was sure.

The one person she would have spoken to—Hannah—kept a strange silence on the subject. Only once did she mention Sarah's current caller, when the two sat with Ellen Winston, planning the children's Christmas program for church.

"I don't know, Sarah," Ellen said. "This would be a wonderful song for the angels to come in by, but I don't know if I can master it." She shook her head at the difficult piece of music before her.

"But you must! I can't sing it! Angels have to appear to a soprano voice—a nice high, sweet sound. That's you, Ellen."

"Well, perhaps if you could come over to go through it with me. Maybe tomorrow night after supper you could stop in and we'd. . . ." She stopped, realizing at least one person in her house would rather avoid such a visit.

"I. . .I can't come tomorrow. We'll have company." Sarah didn't understand why she should feel so uncomfortable talking to Ellen about Glenn.

"Oh. Yes. I had heard you had a caller. Of course he would be coming. Some other time, maybe. We've got weeks."

"After church?" suggested Sarah.

"Yes, that would work fine." A minute or two of silence elapsed. "Sarah, do you really like him?" Ellen finally asked quietly.

"Who? Oh, Glenn, you mean? Well I. . .he's very nice. And handsome. And. . .and. . ." What else was he? For the life of her, Sarah couldn't think of any better description. "I. . .I don't really know him well enough yet to say."

"Oh. I just thought. . .I mean we thought. . .um. . . ."

Hannah broke in to save the flustered girl. "Poor Sarah's already bothered enough by gossip. Let's let this be the one place she's left alone."

Walking home, Sarah's conscience needled her. "I've been seeing him for six weeks now. That should be long enough to know something. Why is it I still can't say anymore than 'he's nice'?

I wish Hannah would talk to me about it—I could use a best friend's advice," she said to the dirt road. Instead, she looked up to the clouds. "What do you think, Mama? Is it my fault, or is he just not interesting?" She reviewed in her mind some of her conversations with Glenn.

Once they had gone at dusk to overlook the river. "Isn't it awe inspiring?" she had asked. The setting sun had exploded, shimmering sparks of water everywhere. "Something so beautiful and still so strong."

"Ah, but not as beautiful as you, my dear," he had said, picking a particularly dramatic whirl of colored leaves from an overhanging tree and placing them in her hair.

She had smiled and allowed him to take her hand, but somehow the compliment hadn't found its mark in her heart. *He said the same thing last time, too,* she'd found herself thinking, and then had gotten annoyed at herself for finding fault with such perfect manners.

Another time, early in their visits, she had asked the most important question on her heart. "Do you go to church?"

"Of course," he had replied, "We've always gone to church."

"Well, what do you believe about God? Is He important to you?"

"Sure. Our family prays every day. We go to church. We live right by God. And we say we're sorry when we don't," he had added with a boyish grin. Margaret had interrupted them then, and they'd never returned to serious discussion.

Sarah's mind returned to the road before her. *Perhaps I should try harder,* she thought. *Maybe I ought to just ask more questions— get him to talk about more serious things. I'll start tomorrow!* she decided firmly. *I'm sure then I'll have a better idea of how I feel.*

She found her chance the following evening when Papa and Margaret left them alone in the parlor. "Wasn't it lonely growing up without a mother?" she began. "I know it was so hard for me—and I was almost grown already when she died."

"Not really. Of course, I missed her at first. But I have two older sisters who were always around. And a place that big always has a lot of people coming and going."

"Yes, I imagine so. We always had a busy house too. But busyness isn't the same as, well, togetherness." She thought wistfully of the quiet times her mama had pulled her away from the household bustle to just curl up and share by themselves.

He shrugged. "I had a lot of people caring for me. Course, things are different now. Now that I'm the master, I've got a lot of other responsibilities to think about."

"Like what?" Maybe, she thought, if she let him choose the subject he would discuss things more thoughtfully.

"Like. . .the fact that the house hasn't had a mistress in some time. I'm realizing now—now that I'm in charge—how much it needs one. Someone who can handle all those household details." He looked at her with raised eyebrows. She stood quickly, realizing where this conversation was leading. "And someone who's pretty to look at wouldn't hurt either," he added.

Sarah paced to the other side of the room. *I'm the one who wanted serious conversation,* she told herself. *But this wasn't what I expected!* She felt a small burst of anger surface. "Is that what you're looking for now then? Someone who meets those qualifications?"

"Yes. I need someone just perfect for the position."

"Then I suggest," she said sweetly through clenched teeth, "that you hire a pretty, young housekeeper. Good night, Mr. Morris. I believe I'm tired." Sarah spun out of the room and up the stairs, not stopping until she slammed her bedroom door. She leaned against it a few moments to catch her breath and her composure. "Well, I did try. And now I know why he's not at all interesting. He's not interested in me. He only wants someone to. . .to fill a position. It's a wonder he didn't just advertise and take applications!" She stormed through her nightly routine, throwing clothes in all directions in a manner very unlike her usual neat self. She stopped and looked at the messy room, then at herself in the glass. "Oh, Mama," she sobbed, sinking down on the bed and surrendering to the tears that came in a great burst.

Tears raged for several minutes, until Sarah sat up and sniffed them away as best she could. *Why am I crying over him anyway? How can my heart be broken? I know I never really cared."* She looked out the window at the brown hills dotted with piles of leaves swirling in the wind. "Because it was all as it was supposed to be, wasn't it? The model gentleman who could give a woman security. A promise of being appreciated. Everything in me said it was supposed to be right. But it wasn't. It just wasn't, ever." She sighed, turning toward bed. *Whatever will be?* she asked herself. *I thought at least I knew what I wanted. Now I'm not at all sure.*

thirteen

Unfortunately, Glenn Morris didn't know he had been dismissed. When he arrived for supper the following evening, Sarah left Papa to talk with him while she cleared the table and washed the dishes. Only when she determined she finally must make an appearance in the parlor did she submit to rejoining his company.

"Yeah, we know there's a ringleader in this area," Glenn was saying as she entered the room. "That much is obvious. A conductor, I guess they'd call him. Someone who oversees all the underground operations here. And it's a big operation, seeing as Alton's a major river town and on the line to Chicago. Those slaves know once they get to Chicago they're almost in Canada. Just a trip up the lakes. And Chicago is so dumb Yankee everyone there will help 'em."

The word "underground" grabbed Sarah's attention. Glenn was talking about an Underground Railroad leader—and an important one. *Of course,* she thought. *He's from Missouri! He must own slaves!* She couldn't believe she had never realized that before. She pretended to be busy with the fire and then some needlework across the room.

"Guess you're happy to see those slave stealers who tried to entice your property north get what they deserved," Papa declared.

"Mighty happy," he grinned. "Now if only we could catch the leaders over here—not just the ones they send out. But we don't know who they are. Just too blasted careful. We've got our suspicions though—and we're working on it."

"Well, good luck to you. Hope you get those troublemakers.

Give us folks who abide by the law some peace."

Glenn glanced over at Sarah, who appeared absorbed in mending a pillowcase. Obviously, she didn't intend to join in the conversation. "I ought to be taking my leave then," he told Mr. Brown, loud enough for her to hear. "You know I sail early Monday for New Orleans. Got some work I want to oversee personally. I'll be gone a whole month," he said, more to Sarah than to her father.

She continued sewing.

"I hope to see you. . .all. . .as soon as I return," he tried again.

Sarah's conscience pricked her. It wasn't very Christian to be rude. "I'm sorry," she said putting her sewing down. "I do hope you have a good trip. You have to take us to New Orleans someday, Papa. I'm sure it's a lovely place."

Glenn smiled with satisfaction. He planned to do some shopping in New Orleans—a ring, a wedding present, and other items. He was sure he'd have a good little bride waiting for him when he returned.

❧

Sarah happened to be at the dock when Glenn boarded the boat. In fact, it had become a kind of weekly habit that Sarah brought something he had forgotten down to Papa's warehouse. Today, it was several important papers she knew he'd need. Leaving the building, she could see a big steamer puffing at the wharf, its tremendous paddle wheel voicing creaking displeasure at the wait. Crates, barrels, and people stood in disorder all around. It would be still some time before all was loaded and ready to depart.

Though she hadn't really wanted to see Glenn, Sarah was glad she had arrived to watch one of her father's majestic boats depart. She strolled onto the wharf to view the busy goings-on. The bustle of a harbor front had been so exciting back home. Sarah remembered the lines of men tossing barrels of grain or gunpowder along the wharf, in a swaying rhythm only they knew the secret of. Fine ladies and gentlemen would scurry to board vessels bound for England and France. The smell of salt and sight of sails always made her daydream of places far away and adventures unknown. It was different here, but still interesting.

Near her, to the left, she noticed a large crate whose address caught her eye. George L. Winston, Alton was the direction it bore in large black lettering. Realizing who would likely come to retrieve the package, she began to edge away. "No!" she suddenly said and stood her ground. "I won't avoid him—it's silly. There's no reason we can't continue to be friends." Reminders of last night's overheard conversation came back to her. Could it be? A ringleader? Did she have the information Glenn Morris and her father wanted so badly? She shuddered at the thought of being caught in between. David was right. One did have to be very careful.

Even as she thought of him, David came running down the steps to the wharf and began looking for his father's very important delivery. Sarah caught his eye and waved him over. "I believe what you're looking for is over here," she said, pointing to the box.

"Yes," he breathed a sigh of relief. "I sure wasn't looking forward to finding it in this sea of confusion." He paused, suddenly realizing that they hadn't spoken alone since that last night. "Thank you," he said finally. Turning, he waved at three other men to come help load the box in his wagon. "It's very heavy," he explained. "And fragile."

"Oh." He seemed nervous, but whether it was about the box or about her she couldn't tell. He also seemed reluctant to leave when the others had lifted the large crate and headed up to the wagon.

"What are you doing here?" he asked.

"I had to bring some work to Papa. I thought I'd stay to watch the boat leave."

"Wish I could. I've got to get that box delivered. Father wants it soon."

She nodded. "It must be important."

"Yes, well. . . ." He shifted from one foot to the other. "I guess I'd. . . ."

"Sarah!" a voice hailed her. "Still waiting here to see me off? And what shall I bring you back from New Orleans, my dear?" Glenn approached.

"Me? No! I. . .I mean, nothing."

"I understand. Rather see it for yourself, eh? Maybe someday. . . . Oh—have to go. There's my overseer waving at me. Must go check the cargo. Make sure every one of 'em makes it safe to New Orleans. I'll be back." He walked off toward the waving man near the boat.

"Good-bye, Sarah. I'll see you. . .sometime." David turned quickly into the crowd, leaving her alone.

"Well, where did he go?" A loud cry she identified as Glenn's interrupted her thoughts. "You let one of my slaves just escape?"

She moved closer to hear, although in fact the entire wharf could hear his angry voice clearly enough.

"I didn't see him, sir." The overseer threw up his palms in a plea for mercy. "One minute they was all here—the next I counted and one wasn't. This fella here—he says he saw him run an' join the line of dockhands."

Sarah looked toward the line he mentioned. About ten colored men loaded cargo onto the boat by passing it from one to the other. Just as she looked, she noticed one on the end cast a frightened look at the ship and disappear into the crowd.

Glenn apparently hadn't seen him. He strode furiously toward the men, yelling words he'd never uttered in her company. "You!" He grabbed the second man in the line. "Thought you could get away? Well you'll pay for that try, boy!"

The man looked confused. "Sorry, sir—what you talkin' about? I ain't gotten 'way from no one. I work here!"

"I'm not in any mood for tall tales—I know my property when I see it!" He began to drag the protesting man toward the boat.

"No! Glenn, wait!" Sarah could no longer watch the horrible scene. She ran toward where he held the man. "No! He's telling the truth! This man is free—he does work here. The one you want—I saw him and. . .this isn't he."

"Then which one is he?" he thundered, forgetting for the moment to whom he was speaking.

"He. . .he got away. I don't know where he went."

Glenn looked back toward the line, then at the boat, and then back at her. "Well," he said, "However much I admire you, Miss Brown, I think your eyesight must be poor. I promised five men to my trader in New Orleans, and he's going to get five men. I don't much care who they are." He and his overseer began dragging the furiously fighting man to the boat.

"No! You can't do that! You can't just take a free man as yours!" She grabbed his arm, trying to give the fighting man an advantage.

"I can do as I please." He shook her off. No one else in the crowd made a move to help the man struggling for his hard-earned freedom. She watched as, nearly on board, the overseer pulled back his arm and hit the man square in the face. He fell heavily at the foot of the ship's stairs and was carried aboard.

A long time after the gawking crowd dispersed and the boat pulled away, Sarah remained there. Her mind could not stop replaying the terrified, desperate face of the man just before he had been hit or hearing again Esther's frightened voice ringing in her ear.

fourteen

In the weeks ahead, Sarah had little time to think about Glenn. Winter set in, although no snow had yet fallen, and Christmas was approaching. Grateful that Papa had agree to her helping with the Christmas program, several afternoons a week she went to Hannah's little school to help rehearse the small angels and shepherds. Other days found her at the church, selecting, discarding, and practicing music, trying to find just the perfect pieces for special services. Evenings she spent fashioning small gifts in as much secrecy as she could manage under her sister's active and curious eye.

Margaret was free to watch this evening if she wished. Sarah sat embroidering some handkerchiefs for Papa, who was spending a few days in St. Louis on business. She suspected, too, that he would use the opportunity for Christmas shopping. She recalled the expensive presents he had always bought in years past and hoped he would be more frugal now.

"Christmas will be quite different this year, won't it?" she mused, as her sister poked at the fire. "Not at all the same as we're used to."

"No," pouted Margaret. "I'd say not. Just when I get old enough to be invited to all the parties—we leave." She tossed her stick into the fire. "Oh, I'm sure we'll have parties but—well you remember what it was like. Who could expect that here?"

Yes, thought Sarah, putting down her sewing, she remembered. Throughout the month of December a whirlwind of supper parties had kept them away from home 'most every night. Of course, Papa threw a grand event of his own every year,

94

being sure to invite all the Washington society editors so he could read about it when the papers came out. Even some of the city's most powerful senators had graced their home at Christmas time. Sarah remembered with a smile her mother entering a spirited conversation about slavery with Senator Calhoun. Papa had been horrified, but Mama would not be quieted when her conscience and compassion were outraged.

"Perhaps we should have a party here then," she told her sister. "You're old enough this year to help be a hostess."

"Could we? Really? And I could invite anyone I wanted?"

"That depends on how many you want. Don't start imagining anything like we used to have, but a couple of families would be fine. We could have supper and some games and whatever else you think. Do you want to ask the Andersons?"

"Yes! But they're only three. So I can ask someone else, can't I?"

Sarah nodded. "If we plan for about twenty, then we can each choose ten people—counting yourself, of course. And one of us will have to count Papa too. And you can't just invite your friends. They must come with their families."

Margaret twirled around the room in delighted anticipation. "Harriet, her Mama, and Papa will be three. I don't know if her older brother will be around. Then there's Emily—she has two brothers and her parents—that's eight. With me it's nine. What about you?"

"Well, Hannah and I—that's two. And Ellen and Rachel their families—that would be. . .hm. . .nine also. So that's nineteen, with Papa?"

"When?! When can we do it? Can I help decorate?" Margaret clasped her hands like a child begging for a cookie before supper.

"Of course you can help decorate. Who could do it better?" Sarah smiled at her sister's exuberance. She had worried that Margaret would pout through the holidays. Probably this year would have been her first real round of adult parties, and Sarah admitted she had a right to feel just a little cheated. *She may be spoiled,* Sarah thought, watching her sister dance around the room to imaginary music, *but she's also resilient. Margaret will always find something to enjoy.*

"I don't know when though," Sarah answered. "We'll make it early so people won't be too busy. I don't think we'll have a tree like at home, but you have a creative touch. We'll make it look festive."

"No tree! But that was the best part!" Margaret clapped her hands with a dreamy look. "Oh, do you remember, Sarah?"

"Of course I remember. It was only last year, you know!" she laughed. "But," she said, suddenly serious, "it does seem like a much longer time, doesn't it? The tree—it would have been right there." She pointed to the far parlor wall. "This room is smaller than our old drawing room, but that's the right wall." She tried to imagine the sight it would make.

The main attraction of Papa's parties had been the enormous tree he always managed to find. It commanded entering guests' attention from its place along the far wall. Glass bells imported from Germany decked its boughs, scattering the light from surrounding candles in sparkling arcs of color. As Papa's fortunes had dwindled, the holiday galas became more extravagant, as if he were trying to deny the reality of year-end records. The tree grew even bigger and the lights even brighter until their home seemed almost alive with color and people.

"But we can find plenty of greenery outside," she said, returning to the present. "Firs and holly and some beautiful berries. And I did save the glass balls, so we could hang them in some of the branches—maybe over the hearth. I asked Papa to bring us back some candles too—lots of them."

"Remember—our cook used to bake cookies—she said she hung those at her house. We could do that!"

"Yes, and make some pretty ribbon candies too. And I'll look in my sewing to see what I might have to use. Let's choose a date and write some invitations now." Margaret ran for the paper while Sarah pondered for an appropriate date. So rare were the times the two sisters worked together and truly enjoyed each other's company. She hoped that would change as they grew older.

They set the party date for early December, and all the guests accepted eagerly. That left little time for putting into action all the decorating ideas they had imagined. George Winston made the job easier a few days later by bringing a wagon full of greenery he had cut. "Didn't know when your father would be back, so while I was cutting ours I just got some extra."

Sarah nearly cried with her gratitude. She knew Papa wouldn't want to take the time to go out and cut branches and leaves himself. She had been wondering how she would persuade him or if she could possibly do it herself. "Thank you so much. He'll return tomorrow—but he'll have a great deal of work to catch up on. . .this is such a blessing indeed." She clasped his hand. "Won't you come in and warm up with some coffee? This must have been a cold job."

"Not too bad. No snow yet, so it was easy tramping around the woods. Thank you, but I'd better get back home. Charlotte will want me to help with hanging things up high. Give my regards to your father when he returns." He waved and climbed back up to the wagon seat.

"Margaret!" she called into the house. "Come look at our first Christmas gift!"

"Oh!" her sister exclaimed as she reached the door. "How beautiful! Where did it come from?" She ran and flung herself into the fragrant pile. "Let's put it up now!" The girls began to gather armloads of green boughs and carry them into the house. "Oh, Sarah look! There's even a little tree!"

Sure enough, a tiny tree lay amid the green pile. It didn't stand more than two or three feet high, but it was a tree. "Ouch! And there's holly too, I've just found out." Sarah put her stinging thumb into her mouth.

"Prickly holly indoors first—that means this house will be ruled by a man in the coming year," Margaret gleefully reminded Sarah of the old superstition.

"Isn't it always?" asked Sarah. "I'd like to see the woman who could rule Papa," she laughed.

For most of the day, the two girls hung and twisted and tied holiday cheer wherever they could reach. Sarah strung swags of evergreen on the mantle while Margaret wound it down the hall stairs. They made holly wreaths for the lamps, setting some of Sarah's dried wildflowers in them for color. The windows each received their allotment of green, and Sarah hung a glass ball in each of them to dance in the winter sun. She set the small tree upon a table in the parlor and surrounded its trunk with a remnant of white lace she had stashed away in her sewing. The smallest glass balls just fit on it. She decided some tiny gingerbread stars and some red ribbon would finish the effect.

"But our old star for the top would be much too large for this tree," mourned Margaret. "Don't you think?"

"Yes, I do. And it doesn't matter, because I didn't keep it when we moved." She wouldn't admit to her sister that she had been glad to part with the showy, ugly ornament. "But I'm sure we can come up with something."

She searched her sewing again, pulling out anything she found in the appropriate colors. While Margaret tied bows of gold and red amid the greenery and on the tree, Sarah set to work on a star. She cut two shapes from some gold fabric left from an old cape and sewed the the pieces together. Then she stuffed it, leaving a little opening for the top of the tree. "Some ribbon will finish it nicely," she said, sewing long gold tails to each of the star's points. She placed it on the tree, arranging the tails so they would lie in curling cascades down the branches to the bottom. "There. Now we'll surround it with candles when Papa comes back, and it will be quite the most perfect tree we've ever had." Standing there with her sister and thinking of the good friends who would share this room during the season,

Sarah realized with surprise that she had spoken the truth.

ja

Papa did return with candles, as well as a few other surprises. "Oh!" Sarah breathed, as she watched him unwind a string of tiny red glass beads from one of his packages. "Oh, Papa! I've never imagined anything so beautiful! We'll put it over the mantle with the greens and glass balls—shall we?"

"That's just the place I had in mind." He nodded.

She began winding the string through the branches, singing as she worked. " 'Joy to the world! the Lord is come. . . .' " She turned to see her father tacking a small, leafy plant to the doorway. "Papa—mistletoe! You did think of all the nice little things. And so you should be the first to enjoy it." She ran and planted a kiss on his cheek.

"Seems we'll have a full house to enjoy it in a couple of days," he said. "A good idea you girls had. Since we're to have a party, maybe I ought not wait till Christmas for two of the other surprises I brought for you."

"What, Papa, what?" Margaret had never left the interesting packages on the table. Now she peered into one of them like a kitten looking for a string to play with. He opened a large white box and drew out a dark red velvet dress. Gold buttons ran up the front, and the full sleeves were edged in tiny gold beads. At the elbows were two small velvet roses, with one larger one at the waist. The full skirt showed a gold underskirt peeking from scallops of red velvet tied up with gold ribbons. "This one is for you," he told an open-mouthed Sarah. She took the dress and held it up to herself with shaking fingers.

"Oh, my. . ." was all she could utter. It had been so long since she had worn a new dress. She hadn't expected now to get one ever again as fine as those she used to own. She looked up to see Margaret's creation unfold from the box. Gold satin with bone-colored lace set in the neck and sleeves shimmered in the late afternoon sun. The wide skirt hung in tiers with more lace edging the layers.

They were beautiful! *Beyond beautiful*, Sarah thought. But, her frugal mind immediately protested, much too expensive for their lives now. How could Papa be so unnecessarily extravagant? She opened her mouth, but a look at her father silenced her. His eyes glowed with happiness—the first real joy she had seen there in a long time. He was proud of his girls and wanted them to shine in this new place. He wasn't being extravagant. He was showing love in the only way he understood—by buying gifts. But it was love. She had never truly realized that until now. Suddenly she wanted to shine for him—she wanted to make him proud.

ꝛ&

The day before the party found Margaret and Sarah busy in the kitchen. Tomorrow they would wear the fine dresses. Today old baking clothes and billowing aprons were what the task required.

"Whew! I had no idea what a chore cooking for so many people was!" Margaret wiped her forehead with a floured hand. "I wonder how our cook managed for a hundred?"

"She had help," Sarah replied simply, digging nearly to her elbows in bread dough. She wanted to add, "better help than I'm getting," but she refrained. Margaret was in the kitchen— and not by force—and Sarah liked the company. Right now her sister stood piping frosting on the cookies she had made. Under her quick fingers stars, bells, doves, and wreaths became works of art. Meanwhile, Sarah's art had been put to the more practical output of the various pies that sat around the kitchen—chicken and vegetable, cherry, blackberry, and mince.

"How do my cookies look?" Her sister dotted red frosting berries on the last wreath.

Sarah looked up. "They're lovely. Quite as good as any professional cook. But you'd better put them in something when the frosting dries, or they'll be hard."

Margaret frowned. "Making them is fun. Putting away is work." She began banging pans and bowls in a noisy search for a container large enough to hold all her creations.

"I've got to go down to the school soon," Sarah continued over the racket. "I'm supposed to be there by one to rehearse the children. Can you finish this bread?"

"How? Can you put it in now and just let me take it out?"

"No. It wouldn't be very good bread if I did that! There—I finished kneading it," she said wiping off her hands. "Now it's got to rise." She put a towel over the bowl and carried it to a sunny window. "It will be warm here. In about an hour, divide it into three pieces, roll them out, and braid them up just like hair. Then put it in a pan back over here to rise again. I should be back in time to bake it." She untied her apron and hung it near the stove.

"All right. That doesn't sound too hard. Um. . .what do we do with all this food?" she asked, looking around.

"Oh! I forgot. Help me carry it down to the cellar. It will stay plenty cold down there until tomorrow."

* * *

Rehearsal was a glorious mayhem of children running all directions, tripping over one another and fumbling their lines. Sarah loved it. "I wonder," she said to Hannah over the din, "if this is what the chaos was like before God created order."

Both girls laughed as an errant angel fell on her halo at their feet. "Perhaps we need to appoint some leaders—a head shepherd and angel to help direct them all into the right places."

The confusion began to settle as Hannah singled out the oldest students to help herd the younger ones and prompt their lines. Soon Ellen took her place at the piano to accompany the young voices.

" 'The first noel. . . ,' " they began, trooping to their places in more or less order. Little Johnnie Dougherty sang the second verse alone in a small, boyish warble. "Did I do all right, Miss Sarah?" he called to her imediately after the solo.

Sarah smiled and rolled her eyes. "You did beautifully, Johnnie," she told him when the song had finished.

Johnnie looked sheepish but thrilled. He adored Miss Sarah. He secretly wanted to marry her just as soon as he grew up.

Later, angels fluttered in to Ellen's solo and took their places, flapping their little wings more like impatient birds than angels, Sarah thought with a smile. "Hans, Sonja—where are your costumes?" she asked two children who stood out in their normal school clothes.

"We don't got no. . .I mean. . . ," Sonja began again after looking at her teacher. "We don't have any," she finished in an embarrassed whisper.

"But why not?"

"'Cause there's no one to make 'em," Hans replied simply. "Papa don't know anything 'bout that women's sort o' thing."

It was Sarah's turn to be embarrassed. Their father, a widower for two years, worked as hard as he could to be both father and mother to the two small ones. Even if he would have the remotest idea of how to use a needle and thread, he didn't have the time for extras like Christmas play costumes. She should have realized that before. "Of course," she told them. "I'm sorry. Why don't you stay a few minutes after rehearsal, and I'll measure you. I'm sure I can find something at home to make up for you." The two children nodded quietly, not wanting to draw anymore attention to themselves.

Rehearsal over, Sarah returned home to find Margaret gone and the bread dough still in the window. Shaking her head without surprise, she set to work braiding the loaf and thought of the following day.

❧

Sarah's new dress felt warm and rich as she pulled it over the masses of petticoats that were currently fashionable. Sometimes she greatly wished the less cumbersome clothing her mother grown up with was still popular. "But I think Mama would be pleased to see her girls tonight," she told the mirror. Opening up her small black jewel case, Sarah drew out a gold necklace with a large ruby set in the pendant. She remembered the first time she had seen her mother wear it—at a Christmas party eight years ago. She had admired it then, little dreaming how soon it would be hers. They had sold most of the valuables to pay debts, but Papa had insisted some of Mama's jewelry remain with her girls. A few tears formed in her eyes as she clasped the beloved object around her neck. "But what I wouldn't give for you to be wearing it tonight, Mama," she whispered. She wiped the tears and quickly put on the little gold slippers she had worn last year. "I'd better go help Margaret. She's probably not nearly ready."

Margaret was not ready. She sat in the chair, fussing with her hair, a look of impatient disgust on her face. "I just can't get this right!" she complained, seeing her sister's reflection as she entered the room.

"Let me help. But hadn't you better put your dress on first, or you'll ruin your hair."

"Oh, I suppose." Margaret stood up and pulled the dress on, fidgeting with the tiers to straighten them. She finally gave up and allowed Sarah to smooth out the skirt while she stood, shifting from one foot to the other.

"Now, sit down and let me work on your hair." A few pins and tricky swirls later, Margaret's natural curls hung in cascades down the back of her head, echoing her skirt. "Wait," Sarah said, "and I'll be right back." When she returned, she carried a few wisps of baby's breath and her mother's pearl ear drops. "Stand up and let me see," she ordered after fastening the finishing touches.

Margaret did so, and for the first time Sarah realized the younger girl had finally grown taller than her older sister. Once more, she felt the start of tears. "Absolutely lovely," she said, giving her an impulsive hug. "And not my baby sister anymore."

The two girls went down the stairs to see to last-minute details. Papa met them in the hallway. "Margaret, my dear," he said, taking her hand. "I used to say you'd turn into a beauty someday—I guess this is it already. And Sarah," he said, turning to her. He paused for a few moments. "So like your mother," he finally whispered. He stood a few moments longer before turning to mount the stairs.

Their guests arrived in shivering groups. "Brrr! No snow yet," said Pastor Meyers, stomping into the house, "but it's plenty cold tonight. Had to tie our little bundle up nice and tight." He smiled at Rachel and helped her unwind the blankets and scarves that held little Luke George Meyers. The babe was barely a month old, and his new parents had taken extra precautions for his first winter outing. His grandmother moved to take him while they removed their coats.

"Oh," said Sarah. "May I, please?" Rachel handed her the tiny cherub. "Ooooh—he's everything that's perfect," Sarah crooned. "Look—he smiled! I'm sure he did!" she cried, cradling him in her warm arms.

"That's not fair!" said Rachel. "He hasn't smiled at me yet!"

"That's because Sarah's a natural mother," Margaret said.

"Meaning," Sarah interrupted with a smile, "that she wishes I'd stop mothering her quite so much!"

"Maybe in a year or two she'll have her own to mother," Papa announced. "It's too bad Glenn couldn't be back for our party."

Sarah's mouth dropped open. She hadn't told him about the scene with Glenn on the wharf. She knew whose side Papa would take. But to make such a statement in front of others! No one could possibly have missed the implication of what he had said.

"Well, I'm sure we'll all look forward to that," murmured Mr. Winston, guiding his family into the room.

"No!" Sarah cried. "I mean. . .that is. . .I—I think Margaret needs me a little while longer." She shot a look at her sister that forbade contradiction.

Charlotte Winston came to her rescue. "Here, my dear. Just a small Christmas gift to show our thanks for inviting us."

"How lovely," said Sarah, handing Luke back to his mother to take the small lamp nestled in a pinecone wreath. "It will fit right in with our holiday decorations."

"A lamp—to wish light and warmth for your home all year,"

said Mrs. Winston.

"Thank you. I'll put it right on the table, where we can all enjoy it." By the time she finished, the others had arrived, and she had to move on to greet all of them. The Andersons she had met before, but Emily's family—the Coopers—were new to her. Upon meeting the two Cooper sons, Sarah guessed why Margaret had chosen this particular friend to invite. The rest of her girlfriends probably didn't have such handsome extra benefits.

"Please, everyone, Margaret will seat you. She set up the table and she knows just where everything and everyone goes." Sarah ushered them all into the dining room, then flew to the kitchen. She would have to be very quick and careful in order to get all the food on the table.

"Can we help?" Hannah and Ellen asked from the doorway. "I'm sure you could use all the extra hands you can get."

Sarah sighed with relief. "Yes, please! I had no idea what a job this would be."

The two girls came in and grabbed aprons off the hook by the stove. "Then let us join in. We'll cut the work in half."

Sarah laughed, "And you're teaching our children math!" she teased. "There's no such thing as three halves of something!"

Hannah joined her laughter. "Just a figure of speech, you know. Truly, math is one of my better subjects. I actually feel competent in that area!"

"You should feel more so in other areas," Sarah said. "I hear such admiring compliments on your work. You really are doing something important in those children's lives."

"I just hope they don't forget it as soon as summer comes. Especially what I've taught them about the Lord. If that's all they retain, it will have been worth it."

Sarah nodded, stirring the bubbling gravy pot. "Yes—it doesn't make much sense, does it—to have all the learning in the world and still not know the One who created it."

Ellen agreed. "Since we had no school before Hannah came,

Mother taught us all at home. She told us, 'Just because others see no need to learn, my children are going to be able to read and write and know what's what!'" She shook her finger and pursed her lips in imitation of a strict schoolmarm. The other girls laughed. "But she always made it clear that there isn't anything we could study that God didn't influence and have some feeling about." She finished arranging the cookies on a platter. "It makes one think differently than others sometimes," she added, "which isn't always altogether comfortable."

"She must have done a good job with all of you," Hannah told her. "Joanna is such a help to me at school. I'm glad she came this year. She's much more of a teacher than a student. And I need one! My fears of having no students were obviously groundless. I have more than I can handle!"

"Speaking of more than I can handle," Sarah interjected, juggling several plates in her two small hands.

"Here—let me catch one of those for you," laughed Ellen. "I don't think I've ever had so much fun getting supper!"

Sarah thought for a moment. "Nor have I. You know, back home we weren't allowed to help. And the good, proper hostess would never have admitted she couldn't take care of everything herself." She shook her head. "How silly. To have to pretend like that for people who are supposed to be your friends. It's so much more fun when real friends just grab an apron and join in!"

With three doing the work, supper dishes covered the table in no time, and Sarah was even able to sit down and enjoy some time with her company. She laughed a little as she sat at her appointed place at the end.

"What's so funny?" asked Hannah to her right.

"My sister's genius at seating arrangements. I'm sure she put a great deal of thought into this." She smiled as she picked up her napkin. Margaret sat a few places down to her right, between the two Cooper sons. The two young men were surrounded on the other sides by their sister and the engaged

Hannah. Margaret was certain to be the center of attention—just as she had undoubtedly planned. Sarah herself sat between her two helpers, Hannah and Ellen. She felt a stab of annoyance as she saw Harriet completely monopolizing David a few seats down. Really, it wasn't very fair to him.

"Before we begin, Mr. Winston, would you please ask the Lord's blessing?" She wavered a bit, afraid Papa would be offended by her request. But she had made the food, and she deserved to have it blessed!

George Winston stood. "Dear Lord and Father, we thank You for an abundance of food to enjoy with a bounty of friends. Let us not forget our great privilege at having both. We thank You for the season we celebrate—the giving of Your Son for our sins and for our freedom. Help us each to find Him this year. Amen."

"Amen," Sarah breathed to herself. She looked at her father and sister. If only they would find Him. How long would it be her greatest prayer?

After the supper dishes were cleared, Sarah left the dirty plates and platters sitting in the kitchen. "I'll hate to look at this tomorrow," she said to herself, "but tonight is to be enjoyed." She returned to lead the way into the parlor.

"You're standing under the mistletoe," Nathaniel Cooper announced to her. Sarah looked up. "So I am," she acknowledged. "Ladies, we'd better keep moving through the doorway or else!" She smiled and allowed him to kiss her cheek before she continued into the room. Unfortunately for Margaret's plans, that smile was enough to keep him at Sarah's side all evening, while the other Cooper son seemed more interested in dogging Harriet around. It wasn't he who stood near Harriet, however, when she paused in the doorway for several minutes.

"Oh, look," she announced as David finished a conversation with his father and began heading into the room. "They have mistletoe. I've only seen it in a couple of other homes."

"It's easier to admire if you're not standing directly underneath it," he answered, not intending to oblige her. Just then, Sarah's rippling laugh at something Nathaniel said rang in the room. "But since you're here," he bent and gave her a Christmas kiss. Sarah, looking around for her father, caught the action.

"What? What did you say? I'm afraid I didn't hear," she looked back at the young man next to her, realizing he had just asked her a question.

"I asked why I haven't met you before?"

"Oh. I suppose it's because I've never met you," she uttered, distracted. "Excuse me, I've got to find Papa."

The two sisters had planned an evening of alternating carols and readings to entertain their company. The family had sold their piano before moving to Illinois, but they had chosen songs everyone knew well enough without accompaniment.

Margaret began on a light note with the new poem, "A Visit From St. Nicholas." Then she and Sarah sang together their father's favorite carol, "The Holly and the Ivy." Other holiday songs, poems, and stories followed, until it grew quite late and little Luke lay sleeping in his father's arms. "You're the last then, Ellen," Sarah informed her.

Ellen rose, and began to recite the poem she had chosen.

> Sound over all waters, reach out from all lands,
> the chorus of voices, the clasping of hands;
> Sing hymns that were sung by the stars of
>   the morn,
> Sing songs of the angels when Jesus was born!

Sarah remotely recognized the words. Was that a Whittier poem? If so, she hoped her father didn't know it. Though the words were innocuous enough, the flaming abolitionist pen behind them was well-known. But as the young girl spoke longingly of peace and hope, few in the room could resist the emotional charge she carried.

Blow, bugles of battle, the marches of peace;
East, west, north, and south, let the long
quarrel cease:
The dark night is ending and dawn has begun;
Rise, hope of the ages, arise like the sun. . . .

Ellen finished and sat. No one spoke—or could. Then David's lone voice began over the quiet group. "O come, O come, Emmanuel, And ransom captive Israel. . . ." The pleading words echoed off cold, dark windows. "Disperse the gloomy clouds of night, And death's dark shadows put to flight." Sarah knew it wasn't Israel's captives he was singing about ransoming. She knew he was pleading for peace in his own country and release for colored captives. But something greater than her own reluctant fears compelled her to join the song. "Rejoice! rejoice. . . ," she heard herself begin. "Emmanuel Shall come to thee. . . ." They finished the impromptu duet, and the families took it as their cue to get their wraps and go home in the frosty night.

Sarah blew out the candles after the last group had left and stood in the dark room, watching moonlight play on the glass ball in the window. "What is it You're asking me to do, Lord?" she whispered. "Why are You not telling me, when I'm searching so hard?" A shaft of moonlight reflected off her homemade gold star. "And what is it I'm so afraid of?" Closing her eyes, she hurried out of the room and up the stairs.

fifteen

Sarah awoke the next morning to a sparkling fairyland outside. Every branch of the redbud near her window glistened, encased in a thick coating of ice. Elfin icicles hung from its branch tips and from all the other trees and hedges she could see. Even the dead grass took on the beauty of a kaleidoscope when the sun hit its frozen dewdrops. The high brown gloss of the road told her it would be treacherous for travel today. Sarah dressed quickly and ran out, still in slippered feet, to view the effect close up.

"O Lord, how beautiful!" she breathed prayerfully. "We never had anything like this back home!" She danced a solo waltz alone in the early morning sunlight. Brown grass crackled beneath her feet as she twirled. *Every problem must be solved on a day like this.* She gazed around her in awe at the difference a few hours had made.

But even as the sun rose higher, she knew the morning's loveliness would soon vanish. Soon her world would return to the dull browns and grays she had gone to sleep with last night. *But why?* Sarah mourned. *Why must it disappear so soon? Can't I stay in this world a little while?* As she felt the water from melting ice seep through her slippers, Sarah knew the answer. No, one didn't live in fairylands. And even in a fairyland, her feet were getting cold and wet. Sadly, Sarah turned toward the house, remembering her problems from the night before.

At least she didn't have to face a messy kitchen. At the end of the party, Mrs. Winston and Rachel had seen to cleanup and had finished before she'd even known about it to protest. This morning she felt especially grateful, since today would be the final rehearsal of the children's program, and she had promised to be at school first thing after the bell.

An hour later she hurried to pull on her coat and give last-minute instructions. "I'll be at the school all morning, Margaret. Papa's coming home for dinner, so you will have to get it. Do you have any questions before I go?"

Her sister peeked into the pot on the stove. "What is it?"

"Vegetable soup. There's bread and butter and some goose left from last night. Just warm it up."

"Oh. It can't be that hard, I suppose."

"It isn't that hard. You're a lot smarter than it takes to do this. You could really be a good cook, if you tried."

"Well, maybe someday I will," her sister quipped, tasting the soup. "For now I'll just be a good 'good-for-nothing.'" She danced out of the kitchen and up the stairs.

Sarah left the house, shaking her head. Her sister's breezy ways were endearing, but some day. . . . She squared her shoulders. "Remember," she lectured herself, "she's almost grown now and you can't shelter her. She'll just have to suffer the consequences and be better for it." Sarah frowned. It was easier to talk about being tough on Margaret than it was to watch her get hurt.

It seemed to Sarah that as soon as the party was over the Christmas program was upon her. She finished the two extra costumes just in time, so that on the evening of the performance, all the children were somehow present and clothed in costumes. Hannah's class filed into the church and sat in front, impatiently waiting their turn. Even little angels found it difficult to sit still so long. The nervous rustle of wings and children enduring scratchy costumes sounded throughout the first few rows.

With his Bible, David stood to read the familiar Christmas story out of Luke's gospel. Then Pastor Meyers gave a short sermon. Sarah could only half listen to his explanation of Isaiah 9 because of the restlessness around her. "Shhh," she warned as she nudged a wriggling shepherd next to her.

Finally, the children's turn came. As practiced, everyone marched on singing "The First Noel." Johnnie sang his solo perfectly, and though he did not call out for Sarah's approval this time, he did look for her encouraging smile when he finished. Then the children faded back as Mary and Joseph came up the aisle, looking tired and defeated.

"No room," Joseph told her as they trudged toward the front. "No room anywhere. Where are we to go? What can we do? To come all this way and find no rest when we finally arrive."

"God will provide a rest, Joseph. We need to ask Him. Surely He will not let His child be harmed."

Sarah glowed at the earnestness of the two young people playing the holy couple. They seemed so serious as they portrayed the scared, awestruck pair. She imagined how sweet, cheerful Joanna would have felt as the real Mary. Probably she was about the same age. How frightened Mary must have been! So much on the shoulders of a young girl.

And what about Joseph? Sixteen-year-old Joseph Dougherty— his name had gotten him the part. He looked awkward up there, trying to fit into his new role as comforter to a scared girl. Joseph was more at home in the boisterous company of his nine brothers and the farm fields. Women and babies discomfited him. But how had the real Joseph felt on that night? He too had been used to rough work—a carpenter's hands couldn't have been soft pillows for a newborn. But perhaps he was a man who took care and pride in fashioning fine pieces from rough wood. Such skill could have transferred well to nurturing a wife and child.

Some words she had heard not long ago jumped into her mind. "If it's the right thing to do in God's eyes, you just do it . . . ." Was that the choice all of God's people eventually came to? Mary and Joseph had to answer it that first Christmas. She always assumed it had been an easy choice to make, with angels right there, telling them what to do. But was it?

She broke her reverie to see the tiny baby placed in the manger. Joanna cradled the little one with tender hands and eyes. She didn't have to pretend to love the little one she held—her new nephew had arrived just in time to play baby Jesus. Sarah looked at Pastor Meyers. Did he feel more keenly, as he watched his own child, what God had sacrificed when He had sent His Son? Beside him, Rachel brushed away tears. Sarah heard the opening bars of a familiar song and realized it was her cue. She stood, a little apart from the trio at the center, and sang with the wonder she felt watching them. "What Child is this, who, laid to rest on Mary's lap is sleeping?"

What child indeed? The Son of God, greatest of all kings, a tiny, helpless creature, given for her. Given for anyone who would ask and receive the gift. She looked at the congregation and willed them with her shining eyes to feel the final words of the song.

Then the angels and shepherds had their time in the spotlight. One of the girls forgot her lines, and one of the boys tripped another with his crook, but everyone made it to the end without too much trouble. Even baby Luke cooperated by only fussing a little when he was put down, so enraptured was he by the children's faces moving around above him. Sarah took her place to play the final hymn, and the congregation stood to sing.

Afterward, she found Hannah, trying to collect her coat, amid a circle of congratulating parents. "Go home and get some well-deserved rest," Sarah told her. "You've worked for it! And we'll be seeing you this week—you're still coming to our house for Christmas?"

"Yes, thank you. Pastor and Rachel invited me, but I'd like to come be with you. We can spend our first Christmas in a new place together."

"Sounds wonderful. Although, to tell the truth, it doesn't even feel like a strange place anymore. Sure, I'm reminded all the time how different some things would have been. Like church tonight— back in Washington I would have seen a grand production with

all the instruments and choirs and blazing lights. But tonight...
tonight I saw Johnnie Dougherty smile so proudly, and Joanna
held that baby just as Mary must have held Jesus. I think maybe
all the gaslights in the world can't compare to that."

"I wonder what Christmas is like in Africa?" Hannah mused.
She shook er head. "I don't even want to think about it! But at
least I'll have William," she said wistfully.

Sarah nodded. "It does make you miss people you love even
more, doesn't it? I imagine how Anne is spending her Christmas—did I tell you she's expecting a child? My first little
niece or nephew, and who knows when I'll ever see it! But
I'm glad you're coming."

ɜ

Hannah arrived on Christmas Eve just in time for a light supper of corn soup, potatoes, and mince pie.

"Sorry I'm a little late," she called, walking into the kitchen.
"I decided to catch up on letter writing this afternoon, now
that school is over for a few days. I got so busy I didn't notice
it was getting dark."

"Sit down and take rest." Sarah motioned toward a chair.
"We're almost ready."

"No, let me help put it on the table. It's the least I can do for
your allowing me to have Christmas with you."

After supper Papa pushed his chair from the table. "And
now if you'll excuse me—I've got to go get something I left
outside."

The two sisters exchanged curious glances as he pulled on
his gloves and boots. Sarah shrugged her shoulders. *One can never
tell with Papa,* she thought. *It could be anything.* A few minutes
later he trudged in carrying a large log with a light cover of white.

"Looks like we'll have snow for Christmas after all," he said.
"Just started coming down."

"Papa! A Yule log! You remembered!" cried Sarah, running to
take his coat.

"Of course I did. Could hardly forget that."

Margaret ran to open the parlor doors. "Oh, Sarah—you did save the piece from last year, didn't you?"

"I did," she answered, "though I wasn't so sure we'd really use it." Sarah went to the mantle and took down the box where she had put, among other small treasures, last year's charred coal from the log. Then she stepped into the kitchen to light it from the stove.

"Careful, Sarah. You've got to get it on the first try or else. . . ."

"I know, I know. Or else we'll have bad luck all year. In truth, Margaret, I really hope our good fortune doesn't hang on my ability to keep a twig lit," she smiled. "But, you know I'll do my best." Soon the fire blazed with the cheerful warmth only a Christmas Eve fire gives.

"You're it," Margaret cried, pinching Sarah on the shoulder.

"Oh! That's not fair!" Sarah jumped, then lifted her skirts and ran after her sister. Margaret scampered around the table, nearly knocking over the candles around their tree.

"Look out!" yelled Hannah, jumping just close enough to Sarah to be tagged.

"You're it now," Sarah laughed. The three continued to tear around the parlor like schoolgirls, giggling and tagging until they fell laughing and exhausted on the hearth rug. Not since their mother died had Sarah and Margaret played the same tag game they had always enjoyed on Christmas Eve as children.

"Now I know why I haven't played that in so many years," Sarah gasped. "I'm too old to run so much!"

"Then how about a game of checkers?" asked her father, carrying the folded playing board to the table. "A nice quiet game for all us old folks."

Sarah smiled. "All right, let's play," she said, getting up from the rug. "Hannah and I against you and Margaret. I'm sure," she said to her friend, "we'll be beaten soundly, but perhaps they'll have a little Christmas charity on us."

Sarah and Margaret set up the pieces and rolled for the first player. A half hour later, to their surprise, the two girls became the first team to move all their players home. "We won!" Sarah cried. "And don't say you took pity on us, because I won't believe it for a minute. We actually beat my father and sister in a fair game," she told Hannah. "You don't know how rare that is."

"About as often as when my brother and William team up against me, probably. I've honed my skills by losing to them time after time," she laughed.

"Well, they do say miracles happen at Christmas," Margaret said tartly. She jumped up to poke at the fire. It was a good thing Margaret didn't lose very often, because she didn't do it very gracefully.

Sarah headed toward the kitchen. "It's time for a treat, I think." She emerged a few minutes later with four cups of hot, spiced cider and apple turnovers. "Let's cook these on the fire and sing carols. Come on," she called, sitting on the floor beside the fire. "We can be informal," she smiled at Hannah. "Anne isn't here, so you are officially family in her stead. And since you're also the guest, you choose the first song."

"Hmmm. Then I choose 'Good Christian Men, Rejoice.' "

"Me next!" cried Margaret after they had finished three verses. "My turn!"

"All right, what do you choose?" Sarah queried.

"Ummmm. . .I don't know."

Sarah laughed. "Then why were you in such a hurry?!"

" 'Here We Come A-wassailing,' " Margaret decided. They began to sing the rousing carol, and she grabbed her sister's hands to pull her into an impromptu dance.

"I guess it's my turn, then," laughed Sarah, falling to the rug when they finished. "How about 'God Rest Ye Merry Gentlemen'?"

Papa, who had pulled a chair up to the fire, finished the round with his favorite. Many songs and several turnovers later, the three girls sat staring into the fire.

"The very first Yule fire I remember," Sarah said, "I was four years old. And Margaret was just a baby—not even one yet. We all sat around the fire—the three of us girls—telling each other the wonderful gifts we wanted the next morning. Well, Anne and I did. Margaret didn't care much yet for what she got—she couldn't tell us anyway," she laughed. "Papa and Mama were dressed up to go out to party, and we were to go to bed soon. Suddenly Margaret pulled herself up on a chair and took her first steps—right toward the fire! She tripped and started to fall, so I jumped up to catch her. The corner of my nightdress brushed the sparks, and Mama and Papa both ran to put it out and pick us up. Then Mama cradled us both and said, 'You know what special gift I want for Christmas? To see all my girls grow up safe and happy and good.' " Sarah paused. "I guess she got her wish. She didn't get to see it, but we all did make it to grow up—and reasonably happy and good," she smiled. "What about the rest of you? Do you remember a special Christmas Eve?"

"I became engaged on Christmas Eve," Hannah answered. "It was storming outside—wind and snow blowing everywhere. Then we heard a knock on the door—and William stood there, shivering, and looking like Father Christmas with all the snow on him. He had walked ten blocks in that storm to give me my present. I opened it up, and it was a little trinket box—just a simple plain thing, not at all out of the ordinary. I got so angry at him for doing such a dangerous thing as walking through a storm just for that! Then I opened it up. . .and this was inside." She held up her hand so they could see the ring.

"And you were very embarrassed!" Sarah interjected.

"Yes!" she laughed. "But not too embarrassed to say 'yes' quickly before he could change his mind and ask someone more grateful."

They all laughed and looked at Margaret. "So now it's your

turn," Hannah told her.

"I remember the first Christmas Anne was allowed to put her hair up and go to a party with Mama and Papa. I was only ten and so jealous! I sneaked up to her room and stole the dress and jewelry she had laid out to wear that night. She went up to dress, and everything had disappeared. Anne didn't go into hysterics very often, but she did then. She yelled at her maid and questioned Sarah and ran all over trying to find out what had happened to her beautiful new dress. It wasn't until it was nearly time for them to leave that they found me—up in the schoolroom. I had put on her dress and all the jewelry and had painted my face up the way I imagined grown-up ladies did. Anne could hardly forgive me the next day—but Mama said she must since it was Christmas. And Papa said he was sure I'd get nothing for presents because I had been so bad. But of course, I did."

"And you haven't changed much since then," her father said, rising. "I must say good-night, girls. It's getting late, and tomorrow will be busy. Don't forget to tend the fire before you retire."

"Good night, Papa," Sarah said. On an impulse, she rose to give him a kiss. "Merry Christmas."

"Of course," he nodded and left the room.

"As long as we're remembering, we should read the Christmas story," Hannah said. "Is that a Bible over there, Sarah?" She pointed to a large volume on the table across the room.

"Yes, it's the family Bible. It doesn't get read much, but. . . Papa does like to keep it out."

"I can see why," Hannah answered, crossing to pick it up. "It's absolutely beautiful." She opened to the familiar passage in Luke 1. "Let's take turns. Margaret, would you like to start? Here—verse twenty-six." Margaret took the unfamiliar book in her hands and began to read about the angel's visit to Mary and his astonishing news that she would bear the Saviour of the world. When they had finished reading through Jesus' birth, she shook her head.

"I don't think I would have liked to be Mary."

"Why not?" Hannah asked.

"Well, it looks to me like she was just minding her own business, planning a nice life, when this. . .this angel came along and said from now on you do what I say. She suddenly has to have this baby, and give up everything else. . . . It just doesn't sound like much fun to me."

"Well. . . ," Hannah chose her words carefully, "I don't think it was. I'm sure sometimes she even wished for her old life back. When people stared at her in the streets. But you can tell by what she said, though it might not have been 'fun,' she had great joy. She knew how beloved she was by God to have been chosen for such an honor. She had peace in knowing she was doing what she was born to do. That kind of joy and peace goes a lot farther than fun, though we may sometimes not feel that's true."

Margaret shrugged. "Well, I can't imagine it."

"That's because you've never felt it. And I think," Hannah added gently, "you believe you might be asked to give up a carefree young life if you take God seriously." She paused as Margaret turned away. "And I can't say you wouldn't, I don't know. Only He knows what would be best for you. But I can guarantee the joy that I'm talking about would outweigh any sacrifices."

Margaret bit her lip and looked at the manger scene Sarah had placed on the mantle. "Maybe so. But I'm not ready to let anyone dictate my life—not yet." She stood up. "I think I'll go to bed now. Good night." She paused at the door. "This has been a really nice Christmas Eve, Sarah," she said and disappeared up the stairs.

The other two girls remained at the fire until it smoldered to glowing embers. "I hope you didn't mind my talking to your sister like that," Hannah said. "I mean, I don't want to poke my nose in."

"No!" Sarah answered. "Please—say whatever feels right.

Sometimes I think people will listen to a stranger before they'll pay heed to a sister or brother. Or daughter," she sighed. "Maybe she's tired of listening to me," she smiled. "And she was listening—I could tell. I wonder. . ." she looked thoughtfully at the glowing log.

"What?"

"I certainly 'gave up' a lot of my 'carefree young life' when Mama died. I wonder if being a Christian and being the stern, overburdened rulemaker might seem all the same to her."

"Have you regretted losing that young life?"

Sarah thought a moment, and shook her head. "No. Not really. It's as you said. There's joy in knowing you're doing what's right. But I wonder if she sees that?"

"Margaret's a bright girl. I suspect she sees more than anyone knows. Behind that careless manner is a mind that takes everything in. But she's not going to do anything she doesn't want to do."

Sarah nodded. "You're right." She rose from the rug. "It's very late. We'd best turn in too." She hugged her friend. "Thank you—for sharing the burdens as well as the good times. You're a true friend, Hannah. Merry Christmas."

The next day tumbled by in a kaleidoscope of busyness. Before leaving home for church, they exchanged gifts. Though it must have been difficult on her modest salary, Hannah gave gifts to all three of her hosts. Sarah received a Bible cover, beautifully embroidered with a flower border and her name: "Sarah—princess."

"Princess?" asked her father.

"That's what it means in Hebrew," Hannah explained. "Fitting, I think. I know how precious your Bible is to you," she said to Sarah, "since it was your mother's. I thought it could use some protection."

Sarah nodded. "Thank you. It's lovely—and thoughtful." Margaret gave her a book of sonnets. Papa presented them both with new coats, muffs, and hats and gave Sarah a set of delicate gold combs. "I will have to wear them tonight," she said, holding them up to the light of the window to appreciate their airy design.

Margaret immediately flung Sarah's gift, a brown merino shoulder cape Sarah had made in the few moments her sister's curious eyes hadn't been around, about her neck and paraded across the room to show it off. Papa's delight with his present was less exuberant. She had asked one of the men at church to carve a sign that read "Gerald Brown and Family." He only smiled and thanked her, but he did go hang it on the front door as soon as he could.

"Look at the time," Sarah exclaimed. "We need to hurry to get to the church!"

No snow remained from last night's light fall, so there would be no sleigh ride to church. Papa and Margaret joined the other two at services, where Sarah highlighted the morning with a solo from the *Messiah*.

Visitors filled the afternoon after their Christmas dinner. First Harriet, then Ellen and Charlotte, then several other of Margaret's friends stopped by to share tea and conversation. Later, Sarah and Hannah packed into the wagon to see Rachel and Pastor Meyers, who hadn't wanted to take little Luke out on a round of visits.

The moon had been up a long time again when they finally decided to call an end to Christmas Day. Sarah stood in the doorway of her guest bedroom, saying good night to Hannah when she pointed toward the window. "Look, Hannah. It's snowing after all. The Lord saved the prettiest present for last."

sixteen

Christmas had barely passed before Margaret began dropping hints about the really big event of the winter—her upcoming birthday.

"That's a beautiful cake, Sarah," she said, as she watched her sister put the final swirl of butter frosting on a tall, white cake. "Is that the kind of cake we'll have for my birthday?"

"We'll have any kind you wish—just tell me. This one, however, is for Sonja, the little girl whose costume I made for Christmas. She's seven today, and the poor thing has no mama to bake her a cake. I thought I'd crush some peppermints and scatter them on top—what do you think?"

"Mmm. Sounds good," her sister answered, only half listening. "Have you thought about what we'll do for my birthday? I'm going to be seventeen, you know."

Sarah smiled. "I think you can trust me to remember how old my own sister is." *Of course,* she thought to herself, *if I were to forget, she's been sure to remind me every day for the past week!*

"Seventeen," Margaret mused. "Papa and Mama called Anne an adult at seventeen. They said, 'Now you're a grown woman, Anne—you're seventeen.' I remember. I wanted to be seventeen so bad. And now I am!"

"Not yet. Not for three more weeks." Sarah finished crushing the candies and began arranging them on the top and sides of the cake. "Do you think you're really ready to be a grown woman? It's not all privilege, you know. Some responsibility comes with the change."

Margaret waved her hand and popped a peppermint in her mouth. "Of course. I know that. But you haven't told me what we're going to do."

"And I'm not going to. You'll find out when you need to know."

She could see her sister begin to pout. "And no amount of cajoling will make me tell you. So don't even try."

"Oh, all right." She put on her new coat. "We're having such a nice thaw today. I think I'll go see Harriet."

"And I'll deliver my cake," said Sarah, wrapping it carefully so as not to smear the sides. They left together.

In fact, Sarah had already started planning Margaret's birthday celebration. She sincerely hoped Harriet wouldn't spill the secret this afternoon. The girl was not known for her prudence. But she was Margaret's best friend, so Sarah had no choice but to turn to her for ideas on whom to invite to a surprise birthday party. At first she had wanted to have a sleighing party, but the snow here fell so unpredictably she realized she couldn't rely on a good covering of white, even in February. When Hannah mentioned that one of the church's farmers owned a pond, she decided on a skating party instead. A few of Margaret's closest friends would come to the house first, for a small celebration, and then she planned to bring cider and cookies to the pond, where everyone else would join them. But Margaret didn't know any of this, and Sarah hoped she wouldn't find out.

She hadn't, Sarah discovered later as they all sat in the parlor, reading. Papa, as usual, did his business accounts. Sarah read her new sonnets, and Margaret picked up Papa's copy of the *Alton Telegraph*.

"Harriet didn't even know it was my birthday next month," she announced. "Can you believe that? Now how am I going to get a party if she doesn't do it?" Sarah raised her eyebrows above her book but didn't answer. "Papa, have you made any plans? Sarah won't tell me."

He didn't take his eyes from his books. "No. I leave all that to your sister. I'm sure it will be just fine."

With an exaggerated sigh, she gave up and returned to the newspaper.

"What are you doing reading that?" her father asked. "Newspapers aren't for women."

"Oh. I'm just reading the ladies' pages. Fashion and that sort of thing, you know." A sideways glance told Sarah this wasn't true. Margaret was, in fact, reading the political news.

"Well, I suppose that sort of thing can't hurt you. I believe I'll retire now. Tomorrow starts early at the warehouse. We're looking at some new ventures." Margaret snapped the paper closed as he came to bid her good night.

"Good night, Papa," the girls said together and bent once more to their reading.

"So, what sort of fashions are they wearing in Congress this year?" Sarah asked her sister.

"What? Oh—you saw, huh? You know what Papa would say if he caught me reading about politics. But it's so interesting. You won't tell, will you?"

"That would be rather hypocritical of me, after Mama and I used to bribe the maid who cleaned his room to give us the *Intelligencer* when he finished with it."

"You?! But you never disobey Papa! I don't believe it."

"I don't think it's really disobedience. He wouldn't actually forbid us to read it, you know. He'd just allow it with so many reminders that it isn't proper that you wouldn't want to read it anymore. But what's so interesting to you?"

"Oh, the speeches and such. Like this one here." She stood and clasped her hands to her breast in mock passion as she read. " 'Rather let us attempt to mingle light and shade, heat and cold, heaven and hell than hope that freedom of speech and slavery can coexist for long.' I like to read them and figure out why they feel that way. Was it some tragic event in their childhood? Some pivotal event as a young adult? And when two people feel so strongly about an issue and take opposite sides, it's fascinating. Someone has to be wrong. But no one will admit to it."

Sarah shook her head in wonder. "Just when I start to think you haven't a serious thought in your head, you surprise me again. Margaret, have you thought what use you're going to put that mind to? Because you have one—and a good one—make no mistake."

"Do you think so—really?" She seemed suddenly genuinely concerned about her sister's opinion.

"Don't you know you're smart?"

"Yes. No. I mean. . .sometimes. I start to think I'm not quite right for the society role Papa expects. But other times I don't want anything else. I don't know." She shrugged. "I'm only sixteen. I don't have to know yet."

"Almost seventeen—almost a 'grown woman,' " her sister reminded. "How could you forget?"

"Well, it seems everyone else has," Margaret replied tartly. With that, she tossed down her paper and picked up a copy of *Godey's*. Clearly, her serious moment was at an end.

Sarah crafted a delicious cake for her sister's birthday. "It looks wonderful," said Margaret, coming in to watch her. "But how are the three of us going to eat that? We'll have to eat four slices a piece, and I don't need two inches around my middle!"

Sarah looked at her sister's slim waist. "One would hardly notice two inches on you."

"Well, I can't afford it. I'm seventeen now, and I've got to wait 'til I'm married to get dumpy and fat."

Sarah laughed. "I don't think you'll ever be either one. That reminds me of something I wanted to tell you though. You are seventeen now, and if you do plan to get married someday—or come to think of it, if I do—there are some things you need to learn. So. . . ," she held her hand up to silence Margaret's mutinous look. "I've decided to start giving you cooking lessons. Call it a birthday present."

Margaret's eyes widened. "That's a present? Enslaving me to a kitchen? I think I liked sixteen better!"

"It's not the only present you'll get. And you needn't act like I'm inflicting Gothic torture on you. I think you'll like it, actually. I'm sure you'll be good at it once you try."

"But what if I don't want to try?"

Sarah put down her spreading knife. "You want to be an adult, and I'm going to try to treat you more like one. But that means

I'll expect more of you too. From now on, you're responsible for supper two nights a week. And if you don't do it, it won't get done."

Margaret looked stunned for a moment. "All right," she said finally. "When do I have to start?"

"You're still not expected to work on your birthday," Sarah smiled. "Tomorrow will be fine. Now go—enjoy your day. Just be home in time for supper."

"All right, I will. You know, I was going to invite Harriet for supper today, but I'm so mad at her for forgetting all about my birthday, I'm not going to do it." She looked out the window. "Of course, there isn't much to do—it's too cold to go anywhere. Why couldn't my birthday be in May, like yours?"

"What? And wait another three months to turn seventeen? How horrible!" Sarah laughed.

Margaret shrugged. "I guess I'll go up and read something. Or maybe I could get to the store. . . ." She went off, discussing with herself all her options for the day.

In the end, Margaret decided to remain home, so it was she who opened the door to four smiling friends later that evening.

"Happy birthday!" they shouted. "Are we on time?"

"Time for what?"

Sarah peeked around the hall. "Yes. You're right on time. Come in. Take off all those wraps." She helped unbundle the birthday guests and sent them into the dining room.

"You invited them?" Margaret asked.

Sarah put her arm around her sister. "Looks like we won't have to eat all that cake ourselves after all. Your friends have saved our waistlines." True to her words, they devoured the cake in very little time.

"Here," said Harriet when the plates were cleared. "Open my present now. I can't wait to see if you like it." She pulled a small oblong package from the pile of gifts. Margaret tore open the box and removed a gold, heart-shaped locket pin. "So you can always keep some memento of your best friend," Harriet announced. "Or of someone else special," she added, giggling.

"Thank you." Margaret got up and kissed her cheek. "I do like it. I'll wear it right now." She pinned it on the new Christmas dress she had worn for the occasion. Margaret smiled and oohed and laughed over the other three girls' gifts—a tinkly glass bell, a book of Scott's poems, and a box of chocolate candies. "Oh, my, I'm to eat this after that cake? I think I'll at least wait till tomorrow," she laughed. Only a few seconds passed, however, before she popped one into her mouth.

Sarah's present came next. "Great American Speeches," Margaret read from the cover of the book she unwrapped.

"What? A book of speeches? What foolishness is that?" Papa asked.

Margaret smiled, looking at her sister. "She knew it would appeal to my dramatic flair, Papa. Perhaps I can recite them to you on long winter evenings." She flung one arm out and clasped the other to her heart. " 'The quality of mercy is not strained; it droppeth as the gentle rain from heaven upon the place beneath . . . .' That won't be in there, of course. Shakespeare wasn't American, as far as I know. Thank you Sarah," she said. "You know I'll enjoy it."

"Maybe we'll even get to discuss the most interesting ones," Sarah said, squeezing her sister's hand.

"Enough," Papa said, waving his hand. "You girls get some odd starts sometimes. Open your last gift, Margaret."

The final box contained a simple gold chain. "It's. . .lovely, Papa," Margaret said, a little surprised. The gift certainly didn't reflect his usual extravagant tastes.

"It's meant for this," he said, pulling something from inside his coat. All six girls gasped at the emerald pendant he set before her on the table. "I saved it from out of your mother's things. Sarah and Anne got the rest—but this I kept for you."

Sarah nodded. "The perfect one," she said when she could speak again. "I've been thinking she ought to have some of those things. Here, Margaret, let me fasten it on you." Her stunned sister made no move to stop or help her. "You've rendered her speechless, Papa," Sarah quipped. "Not an easy thing to do."

Margaret looked up. "I. . .I've been wishing. . .thinking. . .I wanted something that was hers. . .to remember. I was too young to think of it then. . . ." she held up the pendant to look at it. "Thank you." She suddenly flung herself at her father and hugged him tightly. "Thank you, Papa. I will take good care of it."

Sarah brushed away threatening tears. "Then I hate to say this, but you'd better take it off and put it upstairs now. We've got a party to go to, and it wouldn't be a good idea to bring it along."

"A party?! Where? For me?"

Sarah laughed. "Change your dress and grab the ice skates I borrowed for you, Margaret. We've got a lot of people to meet at Seyler's pond." Margaret gasped at her sister, then hugged her before running up the stairs to her room.

All six girls plus the cider and cookies made it a full wagon on the way to the pond. Sarah drove while the others chattered happily in the back. Several young people were already gliding across the ice, while others continued to arrive. Sarah noticed Ellen and Joanna waving at her, standing near their brother. As the wagon stopped, Hannah approached them to help unload the goodies.

"Hello! Happy birthday, Margaret! It's a perfect night, isn't it? Clear and cold with just enough snow. Where shall we put this?" She picked up a cider container and almost fell to the ground with it.

"Are you all right?" Sarah laughed. "I should have told you they're heavy. Papa loaded them."

"Can I help?" asked David, coming up alongside them.

"Please do," Hannah answered. "I think I'll stick to carrying the cookies." She gathered one of the large platters and carried it toward the pond's edge, where Mr. Seyler had set up a bench for the skaters.

Sarah and David gathered their loads as well. "So your sister's seventeen already. And how is she turning out so far?"

Sarah smiled. "Perhaps she'll make it all right after all." She shook her head with a laugh. "But I never know from one day to the next. Consistency, I fear, will never be Margaret's strong point."

"Whereas it is yours," he answered quietly.

She looked at him, wondering what he meant.

"I don't know. I don't suppose I've ever really thought about what my strong points are. Maybe I'm afraid I won't be able to come up with any," she said with half a laugh.

"I could come up with some."

The silence that followed made her suddenly uncomfortable. "Then please do," she said lightly. "I need all I can get."

"Consistency—yes, I'd say that. And dependability, resourcefulness, conscientiousness. . . ."

"Ugh. What a dreary list. I sound so boring."

"You didn't let me finish."

"Well, please add something with a little. . .excitement."

"I can't. That, Sarah, is up to you." He arched his brows at her and walked away, back toward his sisters.

"C'mon, Sarah," called Hannah. "I saved a spot for you to put on your skates. You'll have to skate with me if you're as bad at this as you say—I hate to fall down alone!"

Sarah laughed and joined her. "Well, I am as bad as I said. There aren't too many opportunities for ice skating in Washington. The Atlantic Ocean rarely freezes over," she said, smiling.

Just as she had predicted, Hannah met the ice with her backside almost immediately. "I think," she said, "I should have stayed on cookie duty." Sarah helped her up and began to skate around her in a circle. "You're not bad at all! You lied to your best friend," Hannah accused.

"I've really not done this in years. I thought I would be terrible! But it's fun!" Sarah tried a figure eight. "It's like dancing, only with your feet in the air."

"Go on, go on. Go out there and have fun. I'll just struggle away here on the edge alone. At least I won't hurt anyone else that way," she laughed. Sarah skated out into the group, marveling at how naturally this exercise did seem to come back to her. Margaret, daredevil that she was, had no trouble at all gliding into the fray and trying all sorts of maneuvers, though she had never been on skates before in her life. Sarah laughed as she watched her spin onto the ice after attempting a twirl, her skirts twisted around her so she couldn't get up.

"Not very sisterly to laugh," said David, stopping beside her.

"She's laughing herself. I don't think she'd deny me the pleasure."

"Hey!" shouted someone. "Let's crack the whip! Birthday girl first!" Seven or eight skaters formed a line immediately and snaked around on the ice.

"Oh!" Sarah said. "What are they going to do with her?"

"She has to grab on to the end and get whipped around," David answered. "Hence the name."

Someone else was just then explaining the same thing to a puzzled Margaret. Sarah saw her zoom off to catch the end of the human whip.

"Isn't that dangerous? What if she can't hold on?"

"Then she flies across the ice and has a great time. Don't you think she will?"

"I'm sure of it. It's just her style. But. . .but. . . ," she hid her face as her sister grabbed the last hand of the fast-moving whip.

"But it's not yours." Once more Sarah heard a slight tone of—what was it? Disapproval? A judgment being passed on her? As she looked to see Margaret let go and whirl out across the ice, something in her rebelled at that judgment.

She put her chin up. "Well maybe it is," she said, and skated out toward the line. She caught the end person's hand and felt herself whipped about, almost off her feet. When she regained control, she let go with a determined, if frightened, look. She lifted her skirts and felt icy wind whip her face—an exhilarating wind that felt free and challenging. Sarah turned her face to the wind and smiled.

seventeen

"It seems unfair I have to help make these little tarts, if I don't get to help eat them." As Margaret and Sarah stood in the kitchen, rolling dough, unexpected March sunlight rained through the window and played on their heads.

"You're welcome to eat all you want, if you stay for the quilting."

"Ugh. No, thanks. You've convinced me cooking's not so bad," she said, popping a spoonful of the strawberry filling in her mouth, "but sewing! No. Not for me."

Sarah laughed. She was surprised herself how quickly Margaret had taken to the cooking lessons. After her initial displeasure, she had discovered she actually liked turning her creative muse loose in the kitchen. In a few short weeks she had become quite good—able to add special touches and create pretty twists on dishes Sarah hadn't thought about. She still had little patience with the plodding day-to-day sameness of meal preparation. But on projects like these little tarts, her abilities shone. Even as she spoke and ate, she designed pretty cutouts and fluted the edges of tarts waiting to bake.

"I'll try to save you one. And I'll be sure to tell the ladies you made them."

Margaret smiled. "Now who is it we're making these for?"

"The Ladies' Mission Society. They're having a quilting this afternoon, and since ours is one of the largest sitting rooms, I thought they could have it here."

"What do missionaries want with quilts? Don't they usually go to hot, nasty places?"

Sarah laughed again. "Not all of them. But they're not

giving this to missionaries—they're selling it to help support them."

"Mmm. Well, maybe they should sell some of my wonderful strawberry tarts." She put the last batch in the oven with a swirl. "And now I have to go. I promised Harriet I'd help her with wedding preparations. She has so much to do. It's going to be a huge event!" She wiped her hands and patted her hair before grabbing her hat by the door. Sarah still couldn't quite get used to her sister with her hair pinned up instead of bouncing free.

She frowned, turning back to her work. "It may not be long before Margaret is making her own wedding preparations," she told the cooling tarts. "And I can no longer say she's too young." She shook her head. "So why does that make me feel so old?" She watched out the window as Margaret ran to the backyard before running off down the road. The scene made her smile again. *I probably don't need to worry about it too much,* she thought. *Margaret enjoys her freedom far too much to feel like getting tied down very soon.* She chuckled. *She'd have to cook and sew!*

Harriet's wedding was also the talk of the quilting circle. "A fine to-do it's going to be," said Mrs. Graham.

"Just what one might expect, what with her father's money and the groom's too," chorused another. "The Anderson's only daughter will certainly go off with a splash."

"A quick business I think. They only started courting in. . . December I believe it was."

"Well, Harriet's always known how to get what she wants quickly."

"But who'd have thought she'd want a man nearly twenty years her senior?" Several ladies tittered at this remark.

"Excuse me," said Sarah. "I think I'll go see to the tea." She signaled Hannah with her eyes, and both girls rose from their positions around the quilting frame.

"You know," Sarah said to her in the privacy of the kitchen, "I've never completely approved of Harriet. But I've no wish to tear her character apart in my sitting room."

Hannah nodded. "Unfortunately, they're right. It will be a big to-do, and that makes it the talk of the town."

"I suppose I can't blame them for wondering. After all the romantic talk at your house that day about being wildly in love and unable to separate from the man she would marry. It does seem a bit odd to choose someone so much older and so . . .so quickly."

"What a person says and what she does are often not the same, I've noticed," Hannah answered.

"Like me," Sarah admitted. "I say I don't want to gossip about her, and then I do!" She shook her head. "Well, Margaret's certainly beyond excitement about it. Her first time as a bridesmaid! You'd think it was her own wedding, with all the care she's taking over arranging things."

Hannah smiled. "That's Margaret's way." They walked together into the sitting room, loaded with tarts and tea. "Wonderfully warm weather we're having," Hannah commented loudly. "Do you think spring will come early?" Conversation turned to debate over her question and didn't return to gossip that morning.

eighteen

Margaret swirled into the room where her sister was just finishing the noon dishes. "How do I look?" she demanded. Sarah turned for a last inspection before Harriet's wedding. The ceremony would not begin for another two hours—but Margaret, fidgety and flustered at her all-important role as bridesmaid, couldn't be persuaded to wait a moment longer.

"Oh, my." She paused to appreciate her sister's modeling. "You look lovely. That pale green color suits you perfectly."

"Thank you. Harriet wanted to choose pink! I told her I would not—could not—be forced to wear pink. Imagine that with my hair?!"

"Well, Harriet will wish she had chosen pink, because you're going to outshine the bride today."

"No—you think so?" Margaret flared her skirt and did a little twirl. "Harriet would be mad. She sent all the way to Chicago for her dress. She would have sent to New York, but there wasn't time."

"Yes, I do think so. But I shouldn't pamper your vanity by saying it." She turned back to her dishes.

"Perhaps someone will want to marry me."

Sarah turned and looked again. *Perhaps someone will,* she thought. She turned to hide the threatening tears. "Please don't say that. I don't think I'm quite ready to let my baby sister go," she laughed shakily. "You're wearing Mama's pendant."

Margaret touched the emerald at her throat. "Yes. It matches so beautifully, and I haven't had a chance to wear it yet."

Sarah opened her mouth, and Margaret held out a hand to silence her. "I know. I'll take good care of it. I'll be careful.

134

I won't lose it. Is that what you were going to say?"

Sarah blushed. "Yes, it was," she admitted, "and you're right. You're a big girl now, and it's your necklace. You don't need me to lecture you about it."

Margaret smiled. "And after today I may have to put it away for a long time. It doesn't look as if I'll have a chance to wear it to your wedding."

Stung, Sarah looked up again. Her sister didn't look like she'd made the remark maliciously—just carelessly. "I certainly have no plans at the moment," she answered, trying to sound breezy.

"I know. And Papa's not too happy about that."

"What?!" The plate Sarah had been scrubbing clattered into the sink. "I've never thought Papa particularly interested in my getting married. He's happy as can be with the three of us together."

"Sarah, Sarah, Sarah," chided her sister, picking up a cinnamon star from the cooling rack. "Why do you think he brought Glenn Morris here? For business? Honestly," she shook her head. "He wanted him for a son-in-law in the worst way. Had it all planned out. He still isn't quite ready to accept that it's over. He keeps waiting for Glenn to call again."

Sarah dried her hands slowly. "How do you know all that?"

"I heard them talking one day about having it nearly worked out. Papa was thrilled that you'd have a nice, big home nearby. And you would have had, too. He has bundles of money. And handsome in the bargain. What happened?"

Sarah turned to put the cookies away to calm her churning feelings. "Marriage isn't a 'bargain.' It's a. . .a holy commitment. A bond before God that says two people are together forever, despite all circumstances. You don't consult a person's bank account before you marry him; you consult the Lord."

"Well, you'd better not mention that at Harriet's wedding. She was certainly more interested in gold than in God."

"That's not a very kind thing to say about your best friend."

"I don't mean it unkindly, but it's true. Her older brother will inherit her house and everything. She told me herself she knew Peter Harley was the best she could do if she wanted to keep the kind of life she's known."

Sarah sat down again. "And you don't see anything wrong with a decision like that?"

Margaret shrugged, then looked at her sister and squirmed a bit. "If she's happy. . . ." She bit her lip. "I admit, it's not what I expected of her but. . .she did make her choice."

"Would you make a choice like that?"

"I haven't been offered a choice like that," Margaret quipped.

"You're evading the question. If Glenn Morris showed up at our door today and wanted to marry you instead of me, what would you say?"

"Well, he is very handsome. . . ."

"Margaret!"

"You want me to be serious. All right. No, I don't think I'd do it. I know I'm not as careful as you are Sarah, but. . .I remember seeing a lot of people back home who married for reasons like that. It was just the thing to do in our circles. And some of them were perfectly happy, but a lot weren't. And you could tell the ones who weren't, because they went around with sort of. . .plaster expressions. They'd given up throwing their hearts into things." She shook her head. "I'm too good at throwing my heart into things. Lots of things at once," she laughed. Sarah smiled and nodded. "Besides. . .I've gotten used to being poor." She snatched the last cookie from Sarah and ate it.

"We're not exactly poor, you know."

"But we're not exactly rich anymore, are we? We're off the subject. You never told me why Glenn Morris stopped calling."

"Was that the subject? I thought it was Harriet."

"No. I want to know."

"You want to know everything," Sarah laughed.

"Yes, I do. Did he drop you for a saloon girl in New Orleans?"

"Margaret!" Sarah exclaimed.

"Now you'll have to tell me so I don't spread rumors."

"You wouldn't."

"No, but it's fun to tease you."

"All right, but there isn't really anything to tell. He wanted to marry me because I'm a good cook and manager. I wanted more than that," she said dryly. "So I decided on a parting of the ways. Then, too, I couldn't possibly live in a place where I'd have to be mistress to slaves. It would be unbearable to feel responsible for that kind of misery. I think I'll have to marry north of the Mason-Dixon line."

"Well, you'd better do it soon. You're getting pretty old," Margaret teased, rising to go.

"Go on!" Sarah chased her to the door with the cookie spatula. "Have fun. And you do look lovely." She shook her head as she went up to dress. "What will I do with her?" she laughed. "And how much longer have I to do it?"

※

Sarah and her father were among the last to squeeze into the Anderson's bulging home. It appeared that half of Alton had turned out to see, as her quilting friend had put it, Harriet Anderson "go off with a splash." Subtle smells of early spring flowers around the parlor and in the bouquets gave the room a sweet odor. Though Margaret refused to wear pink, she had agreed on a bouquet of cherry blossoms and lilies-of-the-valley. Harriet's arms were full of white narcissus and lilies-of-the-valley too—a perfect, simple accent for her ornately beaded, laced, and ruffed satin gown. Sarah feared the bride would never get down the narrow aisle with her enormous hoops, but she and Mr. Anderson negotiated the trip fairly well—though she did have to walk slightly ahead of him rather than by his side.

As Sarah listened to the age-old words of the ceremony, she thought about all the other couples she knew who had taken those vows. What did they mean, those words of forever and self-sacrifice?

She had seen her father sit at Mama's bedside, nursing her through sickness, loving and serving her in her frailty and helplessness. She had witnessed one or two others, though—women who had walked away from husbands who had suddenly found themselves in the "for poorer" category, as Papa had. Mama and Papa may not have had all the time together they had wanted, but their years had been happy ones.

She looked up again at Margaret and Harriet. *And to think,* she said to herself, *that could be me. Papa would have given his blessing to my marrying Glenn. I could have had that dress and been standing beside my sister. Shouldn't I be at least a little envious?*

Try as she might, Sarah couldn't manage to feel even slightly regretful. *No, I couldn't ever mean those words with him,* she thought with a shake of her head. *How could I say them if I didn't mean them?*

She glanced sideways at Papa and noticed the lines in his face the past few years had created. She had been angry with him earlier, hurt by his apparent eagerness to see her gone. But no, she was beginning to understand Papa better. He only wanted, as Margaret had said, for her to be restored to all the things he assumed she missed. He thought he had found a way to provide for her what he had lost. Papa would never understand that she didn't want that life back again.

But I want part of it, she told herself honestly, watching Harriet receive her ring. *I want the lack of worry. I want desperately to let someone else be in charge. I want a nice, tight circle of family that can't ever be taken away from me.* She looked up to see David glance at her from across the aisle. The picture of him on that horrible evening came back to her—his eyes holding more than the friendship she had always assumed.

No! She shook her head. What kind of life would that be? Always afraid. Never knowing if your loved ones would come home again when they went out at night. Constant fear of jails, or worse? She remembered the Elijah Lovejoy story David had mentioned that day on the hill. The man had left a pregnant widow when an angry mob had killed him. *No!* She shuddered. *That's not a price I'm willing to pay. Besides,* she comforted herself, *it's wrong.* She focused again on the couple at the front.

"I now pronounce you man and wife," intoned the minister.

Yes, it could have been me up there, she thought. *Then I'd have never had to worry about losing anything again. Just the way I want it. But...Harriet doesn't love Peter Harley.* And for the first time Sarah wondered—was the price of security even higher?

nineteen

"Sarah, Sarah, you'll never guess!" Hannah burst into the parlor where Sarah sat quietly with a book and pad of paper. She jumped at her friend's sudden entrance.

"I'm sure I won't—especially since you just startled the wits out of me." She put down her book. "Sit down. Tell me what's made my usually so sedate friend into a whirlwind."

Too excited to sit, Hannah came closer, waving a letter in the air. "It's from William. He's coming! Here! To see me!"

"Well, I don't suppose he'd come to see anyone else," Sarah joked. She stood to give her beaming friend a hug. "That's wonderful. When?"

"He's made arrangements. . . ," she consulted the letter again. "His boat will be here on the fifteenth. And he'll be here for two weeks!"

"Will he be staying with the Meyers? Because he's welcome here too, if you like."

"Oh." Hannah sat down. "I hadn't even thought of that. I just ran right over here as soon as I read this. I don't know," she said, jumping up again. "I'll have to see about it. But Pastor Meyers is closer. . . ."

"And the closer the better," Sarah laughed. "As long as I get introduced."

"Oh, Sarah, I'm so excited. It's been forever since. . . ." She paced the room and finally settled down in a chair nearby. "I don't know how I'll stand the waiting. I'm truly glad I wasn't invited to Harriet's wedding. I'm sure I could have just broken down and cried."

"You always seem to be handling the separation so well."

"Then I'm not being completely honest. Oh, I think I usually do handle it well. I really ask God to give me peace about it and to fill my days with meaningful things. . .and people." She smiled at Sarah. "That helps so much. But sometimes. . .sometimes I feel distressingly bad at it."

"Then you're distressingly human. And I, for one, am glad to hear it. It's hard work always trying to measure up to you, you paragon of a woman." Sarah smiled.

"You, live up to me? And all this time I thought it was the other way around."

"What? Now you are joking."

"No. Why would I do that? If I survive difficult times like this separation, it's because I'm too stubborn not to once I've made a decision. You've had it a lot tougher than I have—and you've survived because you've got this. . .this quiet strength and. . .resilience. You look for the good in everything and take the bad without complaint. You accept the thorns in the roses with grace. I do it simply because I'm just determined to get that rose!"

Sarah laughed. "And I admire that determination. I guess we make a good pair. There's a lesson in that somewhere. But tell me all the details. How is it he's able to come?"

"He has a break from school. And he said something about fulfilling some requirement while he's here. I don't know what that means. It's not a long letter. I don't know much more."

"Just keep me up with any news then. How are you doing in school?"

"The students are crazy, just as they always get in spring. I'm coping by finding activities that use up that energy. Yesterday we studied the War of 1812. I let them write their own battle stories and act them out. You could have heard the boys hollering and shooting their 'cannons' for miles." She noticed Sarah's discarded book. "What were you doing when I came in?"

"Planning my garden. Rachel lent me this book—I don't know the first thing about even the simplest vegetable garden. Like this," she pointed to a page. "Plant squash with corn so the vines will trip up marauding raccoons. How would I have ever known that? And I've seen plenty of raccoons around here. Last year I concentrated on getting the house in order. This year it's the outdoors. I can't wait to have my own flower garden."

"That's an arrangement you did over there, isn't it?" Hannah pointed to a spray of dried yarrow, brown-eyed Susans, and cornflowers on the mantle.

"Yes. And this year I'll want my own to choose from. Some of those I got from meadows, some from Ellen and Rachel."

"Maybe when it reaches bedlam in the school I'll come over and help you. It will be good therapy."

"Do. I've a feeling I'll need a lot of help."

In fact, Sarah met William before anyone else, because she drove Hannah down to meet his boat.

"You don't need to strain forward so," she told her friend, who craned her neck for any sight of the dock below them. "I promise you, if the boat had come in, you'd have heard it."

Hannah sat back in the seat. "I know, I know. But I can hope it comes in early."

"Not this early," Sarah laughed. "You made me come get you a hour before schedule!"

Her friend gave a self-conscious smile. "All right. So I was a little impatient."

"Let's get down and walk a bit to calm your nerves," Sarah suggested. They pulled up at Papa's warehouse and climbed down to the hard, bare ground. "Brrr," she said, pulling her cape tighter. "April still has a good chill in it—especially here by the water." Hannah began to pace quickly down the wharf, but her friend pulled her back. "We're walking to relax you, not make you more excited. Now slow down and enjoy the early spring air. It's hanging on to just a hint of winter, but I'm sure it smells more like spring." She closed her eyes and breathed deeply.

Hannah clasped her hands together and let Sarah hold onto her arm, forcing herself to put one foot in front of the other at what seemed like funereal speed. "It smells mostly like fish and coal," she snapped. Instantly repentant, she laid her hand on her friend's arm. "I'm sorry. I didn't mean to be snippish. I'm just. . . ."

"I know. At least, I imagine I know. Maybe someday I'll really know how you're feeling." She smiled wistfully. A far-off whistle floated across the air. Hannah's grip tightened, and she strained to see the outline of a boat on the river. "I'm afraid it's still a way off," Sarah told her, prying clutching fingers from her arm. "Come on, let's go in here and have a cup of coffee while we wait. It will probably still be a half hour." She gestured toward the small hotel and cafe on their left. She had been there twice before, and liked the owners—coincidentally a Mr. and Mrs. Brown.

It was Mrs. Brown who greeted them today. The stout little woman with graying brown hair led them to a corner table.

"Please," Hannah touched her arm. "May we sit by the window? I want to see when the boat comes in."

"Sure. Course ye kin. Set anywhere ye like. As ye kin see, we're none too busy here. A good thing too, with my man laid up with a terrible cold. Don't know what I'd do if we got busy like, and I was all alone."

"I'm so sorry," said Sarah, sitting with her back to the window, to give Hannah the seat with a clear view. "Tell him I hope he's back on his feet soon."

"I'll do jest that. He'll be glad to hear it."

After receiving their order, Hannah sipped in silence while Sarah studied the few other customers and the surroundings. A scenic wallpaper of Lewis and Clark's expedition glared at her from across the room.

"I wonder how she felt to go off on such an adventure," she asked idly, looking at the young Indian maiden with the two tall white men.

"What?" asked Hannah. "Who? What are you talking about?"

"Sacajawea. Do you suppose she was frightened to go off to who knows where with two strangers, or was she excited by the possibilities?"

"A little of both, I imagine. But what on earth made you think of that?"

Sarah smiled. "The wallpaper," she pointed.

"Oh, I didn't see that," she said, looking over her shoulder. Turning back round, she exclaimed. "But look! I do see a boat. I'm sure I do." Sarah looked behind her, and yes, she recognized the tiny puff of a steamship approaching from the distance. "By the time we finish, it should be nearly here," she said, smiling at her friend's eyes, ablaze with anticipation.

They finished quickly and reached the dock just as the big, paddling *Excelsior* pulled up to the dock. "I think," said Sarah, "I'll go wait in the wagon." She didn't want to intrude on the engaged couple's first moments. Hannah nodded, barely hearing her between the boat's noise and her own distraction. Sarah smiled again at her usually so calm friend and wondered fleetingly what it must feel like to be in love.

Back in the wagon, she watched Hannah fidget up and down while streams of people flowed off the boat. She saw before her friend did the tall, sandy-blond young man with the serious eyes who searched the small crowd for one face. She watched his expression change when he found it. Even from her seat at a distance, she could see the intense joy that lit his face. *It must be wonderful to be able to cause such a look,* she thought. *I wonder if Hannah saw it too?* Hannah saw him now, as he navigated with frustrating slowness between people who seemed bent on impeding his progress. He scooped her up in a long embrace, and both forgot all about the previously annoying crowd.

Watching them, Sarah felt suddenly left out of some secret part of her friend's life. She turned her head away to watch the dockhands unload the ship's freight. "Go down, Moses. . . ," she heard the men singing as they rhythmically tossed an end-less stream of barrels and crates between them to land safely on shore. She found herself caught up in the rhythm and beauty of the sight and sound. Completely engrossed, she jumped at the sound of Hannah's voice below her.

"I'm sorry," she apologized. "My mind was away in another land, I think. Did I miss my introduction?"

Hannah stood there with a glowing smile. "William, this is Sarah Brown. Sarah, my fiancé, William O'Keefe."

"Pleased to meet your ma'am." He lifted his hat. "And thank you for the use of your wagon. Would've been hard running all the way to where this lady lives." He tightened his arm around Hannah's shoulders. "But I'll bet I'd have done it."

Sarah noted that his serious eyes also held a great deal of good humor—and something else when he gazed at the girl by his side. "I'm glad to help." She smiled. "Besides, I had to meet the man I've been hearing about for months."

"Boring people again, eh?" He winked at Hannah and helped her climb into the wagon. He swung his small bag into the back and then jumped in himself. Very little conversation passed on the way to Pastor Meyer's, where William would be staying. The two simply sat and looked at each other, clearly so happy to be in each other's company again that words would have been superfluous. Sarah continued to feel somehow left out, so she did not venture to break the spell. Seeing her friend's happy face, she didn't want to, anyway.

❧

The spring weather lasted, so Sarah dared to go out the next day and begin digging up the tangled ruin of garden. She soon dispensed with the old bonnet she had put on and let the sun shine on her long braid of hair until it actually felt warm on her back, despite the cool air. Pulling away dead brambles and vines, she began to calculate.

"Hmmm. . .this is the. . . ," she looked up at the sun, "north end. So I should put the corn here. And the squash. And Rachel's book said to put tomatoes in a nice sunny place—that corner over there should do." She created a mental map of her garden, envisioning lush, green plants vining over ground dotted with the golds, oranges, and yellows of ripe vegetables. She straightened and wiped her brow. "Whew. But it sure will be a lot of work to get it that way."

"Good morning!" a voice called. "Aren't you being a little optimistic about spring already? It's only mid-April." Sarah turned to see Hannah and William walking toward her.

She smiled and waved. "I know, I know." She laughed. "I'm not going to actually plant anything, but I thought I could at least use this good weather to dig up the ground."

William looked around him and whistled. "Looks like you've got some task ahead of you. Is this the vegetable plot?"

She nodded. "And I think there were flowers over there," she pointed to a spot near the house. "All around it. And another patch on the side."

"Are you going to do it all yourself?"

"No one else has offered," she joked. "Although Hannah did say she might help."

"Why don't you let me help right now? Diggin's hard work, and it looks like you're ready for a rest. Let me take over." He reached for the spade she leaned upon.

"But. . .you didn't come here to be put to work," she protested.

He waved his hand in dismissal. "You two sit and chat, and I'll join you in a bit. I could use a little hard labor. Studying all winter makes me feel a bit—dull." He took the spade and began to dig it deep into the still-hard earth.

Sarah shrugged and turned toward the house. "Then let me

get some coffee, and we can sit on the porch," she told Hannah. A few minutes later she carried out two steaming cups and a pot and seated herself next to her friend. "So," she asked, "how much time does he have for this visit?"

"Two weeks. Not enough," Hannah sighed. "I'm already feeling jealous that yesterday is over and only thirteen days are left."

Sarah laughed. "But they're thirteen days all for you. Except, of course, when he's over here digging in my garden," she teased.

"Ummm. Sort of. There is that requirement from school I told you about. He'll have to spend some time on that."

"What does he have to do?"

"He's going to. . .to do some speaking. Oberlin—his college—sends people out to lecture in certain areas. He's very good at it—his father is a lawyer in Cincinnati. I'm not sure if I ever told you that. So it comes naturally."

"Oh." Sarah assumed he would be going to a few of the area churches, speaking as one preparing for the mission field. "You'll have to tell me when—perhaps I can come listen."

"Yes, well. . .I'm not sure of the details." Hannah reached to refill her half-empty cup. "You're planning your garden? Where will you get the seed?"

Sarah accepted the change of subject. "Several ladies have supplied me with some of what they had saved. And Mrs. Dougherty gave me some potatoes to plant. So I'm all ready whenever the Lord decides to bless us with spring!"

They continued to chat until William joined them and entertained Sarah with stories of college life and pranks.

"You make it sound like nothing but fun," she laughed.

"Well, you take your fun where you can. We work hard, and that makes the other times that much better. In fact, when I get back I've got the most imposing Greek exam to face—I'm not at all sure I won't be defeated by the mighty Trojans after all."

Hannah refilled his coffee. "You'll do well. You always do."

"Always encouraging," he said, smiling at her. "I'll bet I

could tell you lots of stories about her too you haven't heard," he said mischievously.

Hannah blushed. "I'm sure you could, but I'm not sure she wants to hear them. Sarah knows me well enough not to be easily shocked by my rough-and-tumble childhood."

"What about the time we all went out to the pond in back of Haye's field? She was pretty young," he told Sarah. "Only eight or so. And her four brothers coaxed her into a tree by betting her she couldn't climb higher than one of them could. They both went up the ladder—there were no low branches on this tree. Then when she got above him, Stephen scurried down, and they took the ladder away. They expected her to cry, but she was hoppin' mad instead. Two of them started running home with the ladder, so she just grabbed a branch and swung out over the water and jumped right in. Then she climbed out and tore after them. 'Madder than a wet hen' would have been an appropriate expression then," he laughed.

Sarah laughed too. "I'm glad I had sisters," she vowed. "Brothers sound like a great deal of trouble."

Hannah looked thoughtful. "I suppose. But I learned a lot from them. At least I'm not afraid of much of anything. The only girl with all of them—I had to learn to fend for myself or get left behind. I'll probably be very grateful for that in Africa. It will be the best training I ever received." She stood. "We'd better be going. We're to be at the Winston's for supper this evening. And one of us at least needs to clean up before then." She wrinkled her nose at William, dirty and sweaty from digging.

"Give them my best," Sarah said, "and thank you very much for your hard work. I was feeling a little overwhelmed. I'll see you both Sunday." She turned to go inside, wondering if William might be speaking Sunday instead of Pastor Meyers.

❧

For several days, the spring weather did hold, and Sarah dared to hope it had come to stay. But then the wind changed and banished her once again to the warmer indoors.

"Papa! You're home early," she exclaimed. Her father strode into the dining room where she had come to light the lamps for supper, still in his hat and coat.

"Thought I should get home while I could still manage to. Some fool's giving a lecture down in town—complaining about the so-called evils of slavery. He should know better than to come into a good law-abiding town like this with that foolishness."

Sarah swallowed hard. "Who. . .who is it, Papa?"

"Don't know. Some outsider. Cincinnati, I think folks were saying. Thinks he can come in here and tell decent folks their business. A crowd was gathering when I left, saying they were going to run him outta here at least. Hope they do. A man can't even run his business for all the trouble he's making."

Sarah's original fears were replaced by new ones. *Cincinnati?* Only one person she knew was visiting from that city. "Papa, Margaret's making supper tonight. May I run over to Hannah's?"

"I don't know that I want you out there."

"I'll skirt around town Papa—I'll go the long way. Please?"

"All right. I don't suppose they'll be bothering innocent women. Go ahead."

Sarah grabbed her cape and went out the door at a half-run. Was this the "requirement" William had come for? She hardly noticed the speculative looks people gave her as she flew past. A light, icy rain began to fall, causing treacherous footing for anyone in such a rush. Breathlessly, she reached Hannah's home and pounded on the door. Realizing that her hairpins had come loose in her haste, she reached up to rescue them. She felt a mass of wet, tangled hair—hopelessly beyond repair.

"Hannah! Open the door! It's me, Sarah." She banged again. "Oh, please be home," she pleaded under her breath. But no one answered, and her fears became certainty. She stood for a few minutes in the cold rain, then turned and ran toward town.

"I'm sorry, Papa, I know you told me not to go down there," she said, "but if she needs help. . . . Oh, why didn't I ask him where the thing is?" She cried in frustration. "I've no idea even where to look."

Sarah soon realized she had no need to ask. Others hurried down the streets too, excited by the news of a troublemaker in town. She had only to follow the crowd, which grew thicker the closer they got to the source of curiosity.

She reached the open square to see a swarm of people already there, surrounding a makeshift podium. A few, scattered cheers greeted the speaker's words, but most jeered and whistled at the tall, blond man on the platform. Occasionally they pelted him with more than words, and she saw William dodge a fist-sized stone that came from the anonymous crowd.

"The Declaration of Independence pronounces all men created equal," thundered William. "God didn't call us unequal just because one man's skin is a different color than mine. He called all His creation good!"

An angry roar went up near him. "Excuse me, excuse me," Sarah muttered, trying to wind her way through the edge of the crowd. How would she ever find just one person in all this?

"Run 'im outta here!" shouted a man next to Sarah. Instinctively, she turned and glared at him before continuing her search. *It would be easier if I were taller,* she thought. Then she caught a familiar flash of red-gold hair near the edge of the square and fleetingly saw Hannah's controlled face as she watched her fiancé. Sarah stumbled the last few feet and caught the other girl's arm.

Hannah turned startled eyes to her. "Sarah! What are you doing here?"

"I. . . ." Sarah caught her breath. "Papa told me. . .about a lecture down here. . .that the man was in real trouble. . .I guessed it was William when he told me he was from Cincinnati."

Hannah turned her attention back to the speaker. "Well, you were right, but I hope he wasn't." She bit her lip. "They're confining themselves mostly to shouting at him so far."

Sarah looked at her friend in disbelief. Had it been her fiancé, she would have dragged him from the podium before letting him be exposed to a dangerous mob. But Hannah watched his peril with, not quite composure, but. . . .

"He's a fine speaker. I've always admired that."

Pride! That was the look in her eyes. She was proud of him—and apparently oblivious to the unrest he was causing.

"Hannah! Aren't you frightened?" She shook the arm she still held. "Don't you know the danger he's in? How can you just stand there and watch?"

Hannah turned on her. "Of course I'm frightened! What do you suppose I'd do if anything happened to that man?" Sarah was taken aback by an anger she had never seen in the other girl. "But he's doing what he believes is right," she said, looking back at her fiancé. "And I can't stand in the way of that. He'd never let me anyway—and I don't want to."

Sarah stared as if at a stranger. She felt unable to speak a word, unsure now if she could be of any help at all after coming down here in the freezing rain.

Hannah's shoulders drooped from their unnaturally stiff height. She took her friend's hand. "I know you can't understand that," she said quietly. She paused and winced as another large rock flew through the air. It missed her fiancé, but the subsequent pelt of dirt clods did not. "If you came to help, Sarah, just hold my hand and pray."

Sarah nodded and clasped her hand tightly while the rain and the derision continued to pour.

"'Whoso stoppeth his ears at the cry of the poor, he also shall cry himself, but shall not be heard.' Laws that require us to comply with—nay, abet and benefit—such a monstrous evil are not merely poor law. They are commands to deny Christ, to renounce

His law, to trample underfoot Christ's spirit, and to send His flesh and blood into cruel bondage."

"We'll hear no more o' this," a black-haired man near the front yelled. "We're not gonna keep quiet and be told by some college man," he infused the title with disgust, "we're no better than them slaves." Several cheered, giving the man courage to force his way almost onto the platform. Three or four men pushed him back.

"He's got a right to speak," shouted one. "Let him alone. Go home if you don't want to hear it."

"He's got no right here—we say who speaks in our town!" The man shoved forward, this time with several others as reinforcement. "And we think we'll git 'im outta our town—any way we haf'ta!" another cried, generating yet another cheer from the crowd.

Hannah's grip tightened, and she closed her eyes in intensified prayer.

"And any o' ye gets in the way, ye'll git the same!" The first man swung wildly at the small group guarding the platform.

"Git 'im!" shouted several in the crowd. Sarah felt sick at the bloodthirsty looks she saw around her. These people hadn't come to hear a lecture—they had come to watch a lynching. By this time a dozen men punched and wrestled in a mass of writhing arms and legs. Those defending William appeared to be getting the worst of the battle. The man on the podium bent and called vainly.

"Stop! I'll go! I'm finished! Don't shed blood for me—for any reason!" He straightened, and another man in the crowd saw the opportunity for which he had waited. He took aim and let fly the jagged stone he still held. This one did not miss. It found its mark with a sickening crack on the side of William's head, and he fell to the platform unconscious.

Hannah screamed and tried to run toward him, but Sarah held her firm. "No! Let go! Let go of me!" she struggled. "I've got to go to him!"

"No. You can't do him any good right now. And you'll do him a lot worse if you get hurt too. Besides, they'd never let you up there." Hannah turned frightened eyes to her and stood undecided. "Would he want you to risk it?" Sarah asked softly.

The quiet words broke her last reserve. "Oh, Sarah," she sobbed, burying her head in her friend's shoulder. "God, please let him be all right."

A whistle blew somewhere, and Sarah saw the crowd break around a man she recognized as the constable. "That's enough! Clear outta here now! Or I'm gonna have to arrest someone." He waded up to the group of still scuffling men. "I said end it, men!" he shouted. "That's an order of the law!" He pulled apart the two closest to him. Several of the other attackers, having no desire to be arrested, threw one last punch and dissolved into the quickly diminishing crowd. The constable stepped up to where William lay and kicked his still form. "How d'ye arrest a man who can't walk to jail?" he asked no one in particular. "You—the two of you." He pointed to two men who had defended William. "Carry 'im." He turned toward the crowd. "Go on now!" he yelled and waved at them. "It's all over! Go home and find some other entertainment." The two men picked up the one whose serious eyes remained closed and made their way to the jail.

Realizing the noise had begun to abate, Hannah looked up. "What are they doing?" she asked when she saw her fiancé being hoisted up. "Where are they going?"

"I. . .I think they're taking him to jail."

"Then I've got to go," she said, straightening up. "I've got to go help him there." Sarah nodded and supported her friend through the now nearly empty streets to the small jailhouse. Hannah stopped her at the door. "I'll go in alone from here. Thank you, Sarah. I. . .I don't know if I could have stood this without you."

"I'll come. . . ." Sarah began to offer further help.

"No. You've done enough. There's no need to entangle you in this. Good night." She gave her a quick hug and disappeared inside.

ᴥ

"You're looking surprisingly well," Sarah told William as she entered the Meyers' home three days later.

"I had a good nurse." He smiled at his fiancée, who held one hand. With the other, he reached up to touch the white bandage covering the side of his head. "Still got a whoppin' headache though. Doctor says that should go away in a few days."

Hannah shook her head. "When I saw that rock hit you and saw the blood before you went down. . . . I thought he'd killed you."

"Take more than a mere stone to do me in," he laughed. "Tough stock, we O'Keefes."

"You weren't laughing when I got to the jail."

"So they tell me." He sobered. "I do realize what a close shave it was. But it's not the first, and it won't be the last. And I can't dwell on it, or I'll lose sight of what I'm doing. The reception here wasn't as good as I had hoped—but I've got a lot of people to be grateful to."

"I don't understand," Sarah said, "why they arrested you. You didn't start the fight—you didn't fight at all."

"Inciting a riot," William answered. He shook his head. "The law has a strange ability to bend in funny ways on the slavery issue. A man says something unpopular, a riot starts—and he's charged with making them attack him. A fellow down in St. Louis some years back got hauled out of jail and burned. And no one was arrested for it because the judge declared it the 'will of the people' to punish abolitionists—any way they chose." He touched his bandage once more. "Speech is only as free as people will tolerate, I'm afraid."

"But they let you out. . . ."

"Two days and a two-hundred-dollar fine. It could have been worse."

"You could have been killed," Hannah reminded him somberly.

"Two hundred dollars! How could you. . . ." Too late, Sarah realized she ought not ask about where they got such a sum.

"It was paid," said Hannah simply. "Someone took care of it."

Sarah was astounded. Who would have such an enormous sum to help out a virtual stranger? Hannah certainly didn't herself. Then it occurred to her who the anonymous donor must be. Her earlier wonderings about where George Winston's money went now had an answer. Legal fees and fines such as William's came dear indeed. Only one man she knew could afford to be so generous.

"That's the first person I have to thank," he said. "Whoever paid my fine. It's for certain I would have sat in jail a long time if I'd had to come up with such a sum myself. I believe," he turned to Sarah, "I also have cause to be very grateful to you. Hannah told me how you kept her from running up into the fray to try to help me. You don't know how grateful I am you did. Injury to myself is nothing I didn't expect, but if anything had happened to her. . . ." He looked again at his fiancée. "You were very wise to hold her back."

"I almost couldn't do it," Sarah smiled briefly. She felt awkward and uneasy sitting here. The pair across from her sat smiling and holding hands as if they were discussing a picnic instead of a near-fatal mob scene. And had he said it had happened before? Her head whirled with the insanity of this thing she felt engulfing her. "I. . .I'd better go," she said, standing. "I just wanted to see how you were doing and. . .and Papa needs me for some things at home." Considering it was a weekday and Papa was at work, she hoped her excuse didn't sound too thin.

"I'll walk with you a way," Hannah offered. "William needs to have some quiet time to rest anyway. Doctor's orders!" she commanded when he tried to protest.

"Yes, ma'am," he sighed and helped the girls on with their wraps. The two walked in silence for several minutes.

"You still don't understand, do you?" Hannah finally asked.

Sarah shook her head. "I'm trying to, but all I can understand right now is. . .is how I could never stand there like you. To be always afraid. To have to fear every time my husband went out that he might never come home. I couldn't do it. I can't understand it."

"I didn't think so either, at the beginning, but. . .but then I realized that the two greatest things I wanted were William and to do what was right before God. Not in that order, I hope." She smiled. "I could have both if I was willing to give both away to Him in faith. Now I know I could never be happy in any other life. But I wasn't always so sure of that."

"I can't believe that. You're always so sure of everything. But I'm sure of this—it's not for me."

"Sarah. . .do you suppose your father expected to come here in the middle of his life—to start over, alone?"

"Of course not. He had a flourishing business—and a beautiful wife. No one ever expected that to just. . .fall to pieces. But what does my papa have to do with anything?"

"You seem to be looking for some kind of guarantee. Like God has some little spot marked out for you where He'll say, 'This is My will for you.' And no one can ever endanger it once you've found it. But your father had a safe life. He had every security one could ask for, and it fell to pieces, just as you said." She shook her head. "God never promises you a safe little place, Sarah. He promises the grace to handle life when it falls to pieces."

Something inside Sarah began to churn. What did Hannah know about life falling to pieces? Through her mind flashed the upheaval of the past few years. Watching the clods of dirt thud upon her mother's coffin, matching the dead thud of her own heart.

Waking the next morning to face a house and staff and younger sister overwhelming her with their needs, which had fallen on her shoulders. Living with her father's late nights and near desertion of duties at home—leaving her even more alone and confused. Seeing his gray face the day he realized he had lost it all. She heard again the bang of the auctioneer's hammer as most of their possessions were ransomed to pay for bills and for the long trip west. And she saw the huge tumbledown house that was now their home—where the first night she had collapsed on her bed with wracking sobs over what she had left and what lay ahead.

"No!" she cried. "No! Maybe you're right—maybe there are no guarantees. But I don't have to invite trouble. I don't need to ask for more turmoil." She lifted her chin. "I know slavery is wrong—horribly wrong. And I'll do what I can. But that's all you—or anyone else—can expect of me."

Hannah took her hand. "You're my friend, Sarah. You'll always be my friend. It's not my expectations you need to worry about."

twenty

The following week seemed determined to contrast as sharply as it could with the cold rains of April. The last few days of the month sprang forward as if to dare winter to try to blow again. Sarah's redbud, after trying for two weeks, burst into a cloud of pink overnight. Still in slippered feet and a wrap, she ran down the stairs and out the back door to turn her face to the sun filtering through its colored haze.

"Oh, Lord, it's beautiful. It's spring. Finally here. How could anything be better than spring? Even the name is so. . .happy." She picked a small branch off the tree. "But You must have liked it too. After all, You chose it as the time for a resurrection." She sang an Easter hymn as she broke off a few more flowers and carried them inside. In a small white pitcher, they would make a perfect breakfast centerpiece.

Back upstairs, she settled at her desk with her Bible, but the open window continued to beckon. "Well, really," she said, closing the book. "There's no sense fighting it. Why not use the sunlight to help me instead of distracting me? This old desk facing the wall was fine. . . ," she grunted as she tried to push it backward, "for the winter. But now it needs. . .oof. . .to sit over there." She struggled to move the awkward piece of furniture and eventually settled it before the window, which rewarded her with a gust of perfumed breeze. "Much better," she said, sitting down to her devotions.

Studying and breakfast complete, Sarah busied herself inventorying her kitchen supplies in anticipation of the fresh fruits and vegetables of summer.

"Hello!" Hannah called. "The door's open so I'm coming

in." Wiping her hands on a towel, Sarah emerged from the pantry. "You're welcome to, you know that. I'm letting some of that wonderful air in. I may not close the door again until October!"

"Oh, yes you will. Once the mosquitoes start coming in."

Sarah laughed. "Yes, I do seem to recall that from last summer. Those are the baskets you made?" she asked, pointing to the three objects dangling from Hannah's hands.

Her friend held them up. "Yes. Not gorgeous—just woven corn husks. I thought it would be fun to try, but I didn't attempt anything fancy with them."

"They'll do fine. I picked some violets yesterday—the woods are just carpeted with them. They're pressing now, and we can put them in there too."

"They'll love them," said Hannah, putting on an extra apron. Soon the two girls had a table covered with flour and sugar everywhere, while they concentrated on cutting little hearts out of the batter rolled before them.

"What are you doing?" asked Margaret, coming in to nibble at the batter.

"Making sugar cookies. For May baskets," Sarah answered, unknowingly rubbing flour on her cheek.

"For who?"

"Whom," Hannah corrected automatically. "Oops," she said. "Sorry. Just habit for a schoolteacher."

"Whom, then?" Margaret amended.

"For three of the ladies at church. They don't have any children living near, so we just thought maybe they'd like to be remembered too. We can be sort of substitute daughters for the morning."

"Hmm. What are you putting in there?" she asked, peeping into the nearest basket.

"Just some flowers and little things. We thought that we'd write a Bible verse in each one. Something about spring and new life perhaps."

Margaret stuck her lip out in thought. "I guess I haven't made a May basket since Mama died. I never thought about it. But you always did for me."

"And it's always been very hard to run away fast enough before you caught me."

"May first," Margaret mused. "That means your birthday's almost here. What are we going to do?"

"I thought I'd leave that to you. You're creative—and I'm easy to please," Sarah smiled playfully.

"Twenty-one! I can't imagine being twenty-one. That's a long time from now." Margaret snitched one last cookie as she turned to leave.

Sarah shook her head. "I wonder how ancient twenty-one will seem to Margaret in four years, when she's there? She's probably planning just a small family time for my birthday, for fear that anything too exciting would kill an old lady like me."

twenty-one

Sarah's birthday passed without fanfare. She was right—Margaret did organize a simple family dinner, with Hannah included. It was just as well. Spring and another birthday made Sarah restless again, impatient for something she couldn't name. Whatever it was, though, Papa still had other plans.

"We'll be having a visitor again, Sarah," he mentioned one evening as they sat reading together.

"Oh?" she asked.

"Yes. Glenn has accepted my invitation for supper."

"Oh!" This time she sounded startled.

He held up his hand. "Now, I don't know what happened between you two, but I'm sure it can all be patched up. You seemed to be doing fine before he left."

"Papa. . ."

"I'd like to see my daughter settled happily," he interrupted.

"He's seeing someone in St. Louis, you know," she replied.

"I know, I know, but things can change. He did agree to come here."

As Papa had said, Glenn did come two days later. Sarah felt relieved this time when he did not fire continuous compliments her way. He conversed with them normally, and she found she actually liked him better than before. Although they did not always agree on the subjects they chose, at least now all four of them could talk sensibly.

The cordial feeling continued when they adjourned to the parlor, and the evening Sarah had dreaded appeared to be passing well enough. Papa's attempts to leave her and Glenn alone marred her enjoyment, but she succeeded in heading off his maneuvers.

"I think," she said after several hours, "Margaret and I will say good night." She could see her sister yawning next to her, not very discreetly. The two men were discussing the cost of shipping to Chicago, and both girls lost interest quickly. "But you two," she waved at them, "go on and talk. There's still hot coffee on the stove, and I'll fill your cups one more time."

Despite the late hour, Sarah could not sleep. "I might as well put the time to good use," she said and reached for her Bible. "The Psalms are good bedtime reading." She turned toward the center of the book. "Not, Lord," she apologized, looking up, "that they put one to sleep." She turned randomly to read. " 'He that dwelleth in the secret place of the most High . . .shalt not be afraid for the terror by night. . . . Because thou hast made the LORD, . . .my refuge.' "

Through her closed door, Sarah heard a muffled pounding. *What is that?* she asked herself, getting up. It sounded as if it someone were knocking on the front door, but who would come at this hour? *Only someone in trouble,* she concluded, and headed toward the stairs.

"Mr. Brown? I been told Glenn Morris were here. That right?"

The voice in the hall sounded vaguely familiar. Sarah stopped at the head of the stairs.

"Yes, I'm here," said Glenn, coming out behind her father. "What do you want, Jake?"

Sarah froze. Now she remembered the voice. It belonged to the man on Green's porch that Saturday months ago. Jake—the man who chased slaves with his dogs and didn't mind if he killed one or two, so long as the money came in.

"Kin we talk in front o' him?"

Glenn nodded. "He's on our side. What's the trouble? Must be serious to bring you out at this time of night."

"We got us a tip. Could be a big night. Thought you'd want to know. 'Specially since we're kinda countin' on you fer the reward money."

Sarah could imagine his grin and greedy, rubbing hands,

though she couldn't see them.

"What? What's happening?" Glen sounded interested now.

"Want to catch that old man once'n for all? And his boy too?"

"I'd like nothing better, Jake, you know that. But they always seem to be just ahead of us. Never yet been able to catch them with the property, so to speak, though at least we know who they are now."

Sarah gasped. The Underground Railroad conductor—the one he had spoken of to Papa some time ago. They now knew—and she had known all along.

"Well, this time is gonna be different, 'cause we got someone on the other side now. We got us a spy, you might say. Took a while, but we found things out—names, times, just what we need."

Glenn slapped his thigh. "Finally! We're finally going to get them cold! I've been waiting for that. I don't know if it'll break his bank to get the whole family out of rotting in jail, but I'll love to watch and see. When? When is the time you're talking about?"

The two men lowered their voices. Sarah edged closer to the stairs, knowing if Glenn saw her she'd hear no more of their plans.

"Ol' Matthew von Bronne's comin' up with the load of 'em in his wagon. Three o' them he's gonna have. All young men. Makes 'em dangerous to take without a lotta surprise. He's to meet the boy at Kelsey's crossroads an' load the cargo into his wagon to go on to the big house. That's where we're gonna wait."

"Who is 'we'? I'm not interested in the odds of five men against two. That's why I pay the reward and you catch them."

"I'm takin' Abel Pulham with me. We'll jest get 'em to a jailer 'cross the river. Them lawmen there're more likely to listen to a gentleman, like you."

"He's agreed to go?"

"Yah. He didn't like the odds none either, till I told him 'bout the two thousand dollars."

"Two thousand dollars!" Mr. Brown whistled, entering the conversation for the first time. "Three slaves are worth that much?"

"No," said Glenn, "but three abolitionists are. Especially when one is the old man who leads them all. No one better than you and Abel for the job." She heard Glenn slap Jake on the back. "I'm counting on you—however you have to do it."

"We'll s'prise 'em. Like I said. Course if we gotta shoot in self-defense. . .and it might just be our best defense to shoot first before anyone knows what's goin' on." Sarah could almost hear their conspiratorial grins.

She looked down at her suddenly shaking limbs. Leaning against the wall, she pressed her hands into it. Her face felt wet and cold, despite the warm evening. She swallowed and closed her eyes, willing the scene to be a nightmare that would be gone when she opened them. But her stiff bones and the harsh voices below told her this was far too real.

"Too chancy t'let anyone else know," Jake continued. "We can't let 'em get by us this time. We gotta take 'em ourselves. If ye'll be waitin' to take 'em and give us our money as soon as we get to the river, that's all we ask."

"You can bet I will. Then we'll see what happens to them over there. It will be a lot worse than the last group, if I have anything to do with it. They'll want to make a big example out of such an enemy. That is, if you don't have to shoot them first."

Sarah's heart raced as her eyes grew wider. *Giving David and his father over to the slave owners!* That was far worse than turning them in to Northern authorities. Here they would at least get a trial. The worst sentence, though it was devastating enough, would be a thousand dollars and six months in jail. But there would be no fair trial among angry lynch mobs from across the river. On this Glenn was correct—the Winstons would serve as prominent examples of what happened to people who undermined the Fugitive Slave Act.

"Well, I'll be there. You can count on it, Jake."

"Knew I could, knew I could. We got 'bout an hour before they'll be there. Better go round up Abel an' get." He laughed and slammed the door behind him.

Sarah remained where she was for some time, partly to avoid discovery, partly because shock rendered her momentarily immobile. Hearing Glenn say his good-night and go, she finally moved away from the wall slowly, wrinkling her brow with thought. No one else could do anything—there wasn't time. But what could she do?

Without thinking, she began to dress to go out into the dark May midnight. She put on an old black dress, in case she would have to avoid being seen, and pulled her long hair back into a ribbon. It seemed forty-five minutes must have passed already before she heard Papa come up to his room, but finally he did, and she slipped quietly down the stairs and out the door. When the cool night air hit her still-hot face, Sarah began to realize the seriousness of what she was doing. She needed to have some plan before she flew off with no real idea of what she would do when—and if—she got to the crossroads. "There's no time for the wagon," she whispered to herself. "I'll have to ride." She headed for the stable and stopped when she saw the imposing height of the horse before her. She had never been a good rider, and she didn't remember this particular animal looking so dreadfully large.

Sarah set her jaw and led the horse out into the night. She didn't know how to put a saddle on, so it was just as well not to waste time trying. "Lord," she whispered, pulling herself onto the animal's back from the fence she had jumped on, "Please, please let me get there before anyone else. And let me know what to do when I get there." Sarah began to plan as she rode off.

The Lord apparently did answer her prayer, because she stayed on the horse's back and reached the meeting place while it remained peacefully vacant. She rode on in the direction from which Matthew von Bronne would come.

Soon, Sarah heard the rumble of an approaching wagon. In the blessedly clear moonlight, she could see two horses with an old farm wagon drawing nearer. As she came closer, she called softly, "Matthew? Mr. von Bronne? Is that you?"

No one answered as the man in the driver's seat slowed his animals.

"Is it Abe Tanner? I don't know you and it's dark. Oh, please answer me!" She kicked her foot with frightened frustration. Her mount leaped to one side, and she nearly fell.

"Who's there?" A male voice whispered suspiciously.

"A friend of a friend," answered Sarah, using the password she remembered hearing at the Winston home. Of course. Who could expect him to identify himself to a stranger in the middle of the night—with the cargo he carried?

"Yah. Hello. It's Matthew. Who are you? What are ye doin' out here alone—a woman!" he exclaimed as he saw her come up in front of him.

She shook her head. "Just listen, please. You're in danger. Two bounty hunters know you're coming, and they're waiting for you at the crossroads."

"Whew!" he whistled. "And me nearly upon 'em with my, uh, cargo. But I can't go back. They've got my house—the whole town—watched. I slipped out, but it's only a matter of time till someone will be followin' me now."

Sarah thought fast. "Get out of the wagon. If they're really in front and behind, you'll have to take to the fields and go around. Can you get to town that way?"

"Yah. We can find the way."

"Good. Go to my house. You know the old Cranston place? Up Beacon to the top of the hill. Can you find that?"

"Yah. Been to Elizabeth Cranston's. Course, that was years ag. . . ," he trailed off.

"Fine. But don't be seen. My papa's not exactly a sympathizer."

"Then how. . . ."

"Don't go to the house. There's a shed around back. It has a trap door in the floor and a little room below. Put them in there. It'll be dark and not so comfortable, but if you're not seen, it will be safe. No one will suspect Papa!"

"What about my wagon?"

"I'll take it. I'll go to your meeting at the crossroads."

"Ma'am. . .you don't know. . . . They'll be ready to shoot on sight. What if they don't see it's a woman and not me?"

"They'll have to see," she said firmly, hoisting her skirts and climbing into the driver's seat. "Now go. You haven't much time!"

Matthew went, uncovering the three men buried beneath the jumble of equipment in his wagon and ushering them into the adjacent woods. Then he tied her horse to the back of the wagon and disappeared in the darkness. Sarah flipped the reins over the horses, who must have been a little confused to see their master hasten off on foot. Nevertheless, they obeyed the strange woman now in authority.

Sarah was indeed very frightened that a reward and revenge-hungry Jake might not take the time to verify who it was he shot at. But it was not her safety she anguished over as she drove on in the night.

She loved David Winston. She hadn't wanted to. She was too busy trying to care for Papa and Margaret, trying to sort out where she belonged, what she was to do. And she had planned out too safe a future to allow the risks loving him would involve. She didn't know when the change had come. She only knew that tonight, when she heard two men discuss endangering his life, she had been unable to rid herself of an underlying cold loneliness at the thought of losing his warmth.

Hannah had been right. God wasn't going to mark out a little place for her, define it carefully and in detail, and then say,

"Here it is, Sarah. My one spot for you." She had a place. She would always have a place. Whether it was caring for a difficult father or, she dared to hope, at the side of a man committed to God and to His justice, she would always be right in the place she belonged, if only she followed God right there. He wasn't creating a place for her. He was creating her for every place. And He would continue to put many such opportunities before her. She had chosen right tonight. No matter what the outcome, she had chosen right.

" 'Saviour, like a Shepherd lead us. . . .' " Sarah began to sing softly to combat both her fear and the black stillness. " 'Much we need Thy tender care. . . .' " She smiled for the first time that night. She surely would need His care. And she had it, she suddenly realized, for the very song she sang would be her guarantee of safety. The ambushing men might not know the sight of a woman in the moonlight, but they would know the sound of one! Surely they would not fire at a young woman singing hymns while driving down the road, no matter how suspicious the hour. It might also be the warning David needed that something was amiss. He had certainly heard her voice often enough. Would he recognize it and be forewarned?

" 'Blessed Jesus. . . ,' " she began again, louder, and with the full force of her renewed faith behind it. " 'Thou hast loved us; love us still. . . .' "

A few choruses later, Sarah approached the crossroads. She could see the familiar figure in a wagon pulled up opposite. She had only just heard it stop, so their timing was good. Upon hearing her voice, David began to turn around.

"You're not going already, are you?" Sarah called out. "I just got here! I'm not that late." She gave a false little laugh she hoped sounded convincingly merry. Throwing Abe's reins around a branch, she headed for the opposite wagon and a very shocked looking David. "Or did you decide to go meet another girl who would be more obligingly on time?" She laughed again, climbing quickly into his wagon.

"Sarah, what. . . ?" Her eyes warned him to be quiet. At odds with the seriousness of those eyes, her voice trilled once again. "Well, where are we going? Let's be off then, before Papa knows I'm gone. I can't stay out too long, you know."

Taking her cue, David flipped the reins over the horses and turned left, covering some distance in silence while Sarah repeatedly peered over her shoulder to be sure Jake and Abel had believed her ruse and not followed them.

"Are you ever going to tell me what on earth is going on and why you keep looking behind us and why I can't seem to remember planning to meet you on the road at this hour?" His voice rose with each "why."

"And what am I doing here in the first place? In Matthew von Bronne's wagon?"

"Von Bronne's!" Do you know what's supposed to be in. . . ," he began to turn the wagon around.

She put out her hand to stop him. "Yes, I do, and they're no longer there. Though I've no doubt Jake and Abel checked it thoroughly after I left to make sure."

"Jake and Abel? Whoa. For the sake of proving I'm not dreaming all this, please explain."

So Sarah did explain, from the overheard conversation earlier to her decision to hail him on the road to where Farmer von Bronne and his "cargo" were now.

"I couldn't take the chance you would act surprised. Everything depended on it looking like you expected me, not Matthew. So I spoke up first and didn't stop talking until I could keep you from saying anything."

"Well it worked. I was much too shocked by what you said to ask anything! But Sarah, do you know what that meeting will look like? What they're thinking and saying right now?"

"Yes, it will look exactly like what I intended it to. A midnight tryst. And if they spread it around, which I've no doubt of," she frowned wryly, "I'll be ruined. But ruined is better than dead, after all, and I hadn't much choice. I couldn't give you any time to ask questions, and it had to be believable."

David's jaw dropped. "So you very calmly walked right into a trap and planned every step of it." He shook his head. "But why? You might well have been killed! You should never have done that!"

"And if I hadn't?" Her question hung there, unanswerable.

He put his head in his hand, shaking it yet again. "What can I say? I'm furious with you for doing it. It terrifies me to even think of what might have happened to you. But I don't much like the thought of what would have happened to me if you hadn't."

Sarah took his other hand. " 'If it's the right thing to do in God's eyes, you just do it and leave the consequences to Him.' Haven't I heard that somewhere?"

He looked at her and smiled shakily. "It was easy enough to say those words when I was the one in danger. Sarah, do you have any idea what it would mean to me to have lost you?"

She looked down at her hands. "Knowing how I felt when they talked about shooting you, I think I do."

He took both her hands. "Then you've changed your mind?"

"I guess I have. Does the offer to become a wild-eyed abolitionist still stand?" she smiled questioningly.

"No. You're already an abolitionist. And I don't think I'd like a wild-eyed wife."

Sarah's slight smile turned into an absolute grin.

A Letter To Our Readers

Dear Reader:

In order that we might better contribute to your reading enjoyment, we would appreciate your taking a few minutes to respond to the following questions. When completed, please return to the following:

Rebecca Germany, Managing Editor
Heartsong Presents
P.O. Box 719
Uhrichsville, Ohio 44683

1. Did you enjoy reading *Friend of a Friend*?
   ❏ Very much. I would like to see more books
     by this author!
   ❏ Moderately
     I would have enjoyed it more if _____

     _____

2. Are you a member of **Heartsong Presents**? ❏Yes ❏No
   If no, where did you purchase this book? _____

   _____

3. What influenced your decision to purchase this
   book? (Check those that apply.)

   ❏ Cover   ❏ Back cover copy

   ❏ Title   ❏ Friends

   ❏ Publicity   ❏ Other_____

4. How would you rate, on a scale from 1 (poor) to 5
   (superior), the cover design? _____

5. On a scale from 1 (poor) to 10 (superior), please rate the following elements.

___Heroine   ___Plot

___Hero   ___Inspirational theme

___Setting   ___Secondary characters

6. What settings would you like to see covered in **Heartsong Presents** books?_____

_____

_____

7. What are some inspirational themes you would like to see treated in future books?_____

_____

_____

8. Would you be interested in reading other **Heartsong Presents** titles?   ❏ Yes   ❏ No

9. Please check your age range:
   ❏ Under 18   ❏ 18-24   ❏ 25-34
   ❏ 35-45   ❏ 46-55   ❏ Over 55

10. How many hours per week do you read? _____

Name _____

Occupation _____

Address _____

City_____ State_____ Zip _____